ALEXANDRIA'S
GOLD

ALEXANDRIA'S
GOLD

ANNMARIE H. PEARSON

Alexandria's Gold

Copyright © 2024 by Annmarie H. Pearson. All rights reserved.

No part of this publication may be reproduced, stored in a retrieval system or transmitted in any way by any means, electronic, mechanical, photocopy, recording or otherwise without the prior permission of the author except as provided by USA copyright law.

The opinions expressed by the author are not necessarily those of URLink Print and Media.

1603 Capitol Ave., Suite 310 Cheyenne, Wyoming USA 82001
1-888-980-6523 | admin@urlinkpublishing.com

URLink Print and Media is committed to excellence in the publishing industry.

Book design copyright © 2024 by URLink Print and Media. All rights reserved.

Published in the United States of America

Library of Congress Control Number: 2024908668
ISBN 978-1-68486-757-8 (Paperback)
ISBN 978-1-68486-760-8 (Digital)

12.04.24

To Janice Van Havermaat for her friendship and for her enthusiastic encouragement to continue writing on a new adventure in a family drama/suspense novel that has been tucked away in my imagination for quite some time. Thank you.

PART ONE

LAST BREATH: IN THE BEGINNING

Chapter

ONE

My name is Alexandria Tillie Bush, but most people call me Alex. My grandfather wanted my mother to have a son and was greatly disappointed when I turned out to be a girl. My mother nicknamed me Alex to please her father, my grandfather, Len Hudson. Since my mother delivered me in a cesarean birth, and with much difficulty, I ended up an only child.

Granddad was a prospector for gold in his younger days. His prospector's gold turned into a foredoomed legacy for me. My father and I almost lost our lives, and one of my sorority girlfriends broke a limb, her left leg, all because of an adventure that my grandfather bequeathed to me on his dying bed.

My boyfriend, Effram, almost died by what we all assumed was an accident in an unusual incident in the wilderness. One of my college girlfriends and her male companion were horrendously mutilated trying to help me redeem my grandfather's hidden buried treasure from his gold-mining days. Granddad wanted me to retrieve his buried gold that he left in the Mogollon Mountains of New Mexico some fifty odd years ago.

It all started when I passed my grandfather's bedroom door, and waved a good morning greeting to him while I was visiting my parents on spring break.

"Good morning, Granddad. How are you doing today?" I greeted him excitedly, for I was just getting ready to leave in my new Ford pickup truck that he had given me for my twenty-first birthday.

My grandfather lay quietly on his bed in his daughter's house, my parent's home, dying of old age. We all live in Glenwood, on a ranch in a small town between Reserve and Silver City in New Mexico, which is on the outskirts of four mountain ranges: The Mogollon Mountains, San Francisco Mountains, Tularosa Mountains, and the Elk Mountains. The Gallo and Mangas Mountains skirt the northern mountain ranges, and the Mimbres Mountains skirt the southern range. All these mountains are right smack in the middle of the Apache National Forest, and only a hop, skip, and a jump into the Gila National Wilderness, not far from the Gila Cliff Dwellings National Monument.

Glenwood is about sixty miles Northwest of Silver City, and travel time of 240 miles South of Albuquerque via the Interstate 25. The countryside is desert and mostly barren with some cactus, yucca, and mesquite bushes for a bit of scenery, until you reach the mountain ranges in the magnificent Apache and Gila Forests on Highway 180. Then the terrain turns into a beautiful landscape of evergreen trees and piñon trees with rolling hills and an abundance of wildlife. The Apache and Gila National Forests are home to the antelope, elk, deer, black bear, mountain lion, cotton tail and mule deer rabbits, and too many wild turkeys. The magnificent mountains of New Mexico are also the habitat for both javelinas and wild boars, which are known to be very vigilant, and sometimes vicious, nocturnal and diurnal animals.

My mother married into the Bush family, my father's family, who was one of the first founding families of Glenwood Springs, New Mexico, since 1878. After the gold rush craze ended, the town became known as Glenwood. The township had dropped the *Springs* from the courtlier title.

Mary Tillie Bush is my mother's full name. She was named after her mother, Mary, who was my grandfather's wife, and Tillie, who was my grandfather's aunt, who raised him to the age of nineteen. That was when Len Hudson ran away to become a gold miner.

Len Hudson, now eighty-nine years old, lay helpless in his bed. He watched the days go by unable to move freely, for his body was withering away. He once was a sturdy big man, usually weighing in at 230 pounds. He was fit and rowdy in his younger days, mostly muscle, not fat, but today he was slowly dying in his bed, and he wanted to share his life's story with me.

"I'm feeling a bit poorly today, Alex. Not one of my better days. Do you have a moment to spare for your old granddad? I have a story to tell you, and I promise you, it will be a good one. It may even benefit you if you act upon the adventure after my tale."

My grandfather was grinning in his bed as he struggled to prop himself up with pillows to relate his story to me. My grandfather truly believed that my life would have changed dramatically from this adventure that he planned to offer me at the end of his story. The change would be for my better or for my worst, according to how I chose to experience the mountains on my quest, if I did take up his proposal. What my grandfather didn't realize was that this adventure would turn out to be the biggest nightmare of my life.

My grandfather continued his narrative story after he took a deep breath.

"I had offered this same adventure to your mother when she was about your age. I didn't go into great detail as I am about to tell you. I felt that this story, the story that I'm about to share with you, well, I didn't think it would interest your mother as I believe, and as I hope, will interest you. Your mother chose to elope with your dad, and as you know, your mother is not the adventurous type. She wanted to have a child of her own, and she got pregnant with you right after your mother and your father were married."

I had been intrigued with my grandfather all my life. He always had great tales to tell me about his adventures when he was younger, but he never talked about his early life. Never about his family, or how he got his money, or how he met my grandmother, Mary Ann Strauss. I pulled up a chair near my grandfather's bed, and I helped him with his pillows before I sat on the hard oak chair. I sat there quietly for the longest time and waited for him to continue as he seemed fixed in his gaze on me.

Len Hudson stared at his granddaughter with loving admiration. Len and Alex both sat quietly for a short pause as Len reflected on his granddaughter's character.

This young woman always has time for me, Len Hudson thought. *She is a pretty girl, yet a bit tomboy, very independent more like a frontierswoman. Maybe this aspect of her personality will tempt her to accept my quest to find my buried gold.* He continued his thoughts questionably but with great anticipation.

Len continued his thought of Alex as he lovingly gazed over his granddaughter's appearance. He sincerely loved his granddaughter's long, wavy black hair, and her deep, mesmeric royal blue eyes.

Oh, how she looks so much like her grandmother, my dearly beloved Mary, Len thought with a nostalgic pain of loneliness for his deceased wife. *I've missed you, Mary. I've missed you so much, my beloved. It was hard to raise our daughter alone when you left me, but I always felt your presence when I needed you.*

Len stared at Alex as he pondered on her feminine attributes, all while his heart ached for his deceased dearly beloved.

Alexandria was tall, taller than him only by half an inch, and he was at least five-foot-ten, in his budding days. She weighed about 120 pounds, soaking wet. She was also well endowed like her mother and grandmother before her. Even though she was voluptuous and shapely, she was physically strong and street-smart, as well as book smart. Alex graduated top of her high school class and received a scholarship for college. She was home for summer break and had just completed her second year at the New Mexico State University in Las Cruces. She could have accepted the proposals for other colleges in the east that her mother was pushing her to accept, but she had too much country girl in her, and every time she thought of leaving her family and her precious mountains of the Apache and Gila Wilderness, well, it was more than she could bare.

Alex was always on a horse riding a ridge through the rough and rugged mountain ranges. She loved every horse on their equestrian ranch. Grooming them was a pleasure for her, not a chore, after her schoolwork was done. Pulling ticks from the horses' ears; brushing

Avon's Skin-So-Soft oil into the horse's hide to keep the flies, mosquitoes, and ticks from biting them and laying pupa eggs near their eyes or open sores; and brushing and braiding their manes were just some of the many nonchore equine activities that she could have done for hours.

Len shook his head when Alex interrupted his flashback memories of his precious granddaughter growing up.

"Sure Granddad, I'm here for you. What do you want to tell me?" Alex shifted her weight onto the two back legs of the hard oak chair in her grandfather's bedroom as she spoke. She was eager to pass the time with another tale. He had so many of them, and they were all adventurous.

Granddad was always active when he was younger. Nothing stopped him short of fulfilling his expectations, nothing now, but his old age.

"Well, I would like to share my life's tale with you, if you don't mind. There is one event that occurred in my life that I want to hand over to you. That is, after you have heard my accounts, and what I have done with some treasures that I accumulated in my youth.

"I'm leaving them all to you, Alex. You'll have to go get it. I'll tell you where it's hid, but you will have to take the adventure to find it."

Len Hudson closed his eyes to let his granddaughter absorb his words, and he hoped that she would think of it as a thrilling new adventure in her life. Like the adventure that changed his life when he was younger. Len Hudson had no knowledge of the terror that was to follow his granddaughter into the Gila Wilderness of the Mogollon Mountains.

Len purposely lay quietly for a while to collect his thoughts, as he watched his granddaughter nestle herself comfortably in the hard oak chair by his bed. Slowly he opened his eyes and started to recount his life's story.

"I was born in the early nineteen hundreds on West Randolph Street in the loop community area of Chicago, Illinois, at Hotel Sherman, so I've been told. My mother and father both worked there, that's how they met."

"I used to play on the Cortland Street Bridge when I was a young lad. It was a swing bridge that connected the west side over the Chicago River that emptied into Lake Michigan. I remember seeing many horse-drawn wagons that were filled with steel workers and packing plant employees."

Granddad stopped for a brief second to shuffle his weight in his bed, and then he continued.

"There were rows of new, shiny, black automobiles—General Motors, Fords, and Chryslers—that were ready to cross when the bridge finished its cycle to close the wings of the steam-powered bridge. There were people on bicycles, and hundreds of pedestrians waiting and watching the counterweights, the huge gears, and the steam motors that rotated when the swing bridge was closing. The grinding noise of metal rubbing against metal was so loud that the live chickens in the butcher shops would squawk and clamor with fright. Wild pigeons would flutter in waves nervously over the bridge. Everyone wanted to cross in a hurry early each morning. Countless horses whinnied raucously, while the drivers from the multiple vehicles pressed their brassy horns. There were so many pedestrians talking all at the same time as they waited for the swing bridge to close. It was difficult to distinguish one conversation from another, unless you were standing directly opposite the person who was speaking. One of the most spectacular views I had ever seen in my life was that swing bridge pivoting to allow boats to pass through on the Chicago River. I tell you; it was an amazing sight."

Granddad stopped for a moment to recollect his thoughts, and then continued to recount his youth.

"I was ten years old when my father was killed in an accident by two horse-drawn streetcars on Madison Street between South Canal and South Clinton Street. One of those damn things toppled over and crushed my father when they collided. My mother was devastated, and she had a hard time coping after that. Life wasn't easy in those days. We didn't have all the luxuries that you have today. I don't believe that any of today's luxuries would have helped my mother in any way."

Granddad stopped again, inhaled a huge breath, and stared directly into my eyes to see if I was paying attention to his story. He used to do that when I was younger to make sure he had a captive audience. I do believe that this time he probably stopped to give his respect to both his parents who had died so many years ago. I could see that his eyes were becoming glassy, and a tear may have been forming, but granddad wiped it away quickly before his emotions were out of control.

Granddad continued, "Aunt Tillie, my mother's older sister by eight years, convinced my mother to let me move in with her since my mother couldn't and wouldn't care for me anymore. The day Aunt Tillie and I left to go to her mini farm was the last time I ever saw my mother. My Aunt Tillie said that my mother died a lonely woman. She wouldn't tell me anymore than that. I'm not sure if my mother killed herself, or just up and died as a lonely woman. It can happen, I heard, dying of loneliness."

I watched my grandfather relate his life's history. This was a different tale than his normal stories. This time, granddad was telling me about his early life, about my great aunt Tillie. I heard about Great-Aunt Tillie a few times before, but never in detail, and granddad never talked about his wife, my grandmother, Mary Ann Strauss. He said it was just too painful to talk about her, since she had died.

I leaned forward to draw the blanket over Granddad's arms when I noticed him shivering with a chill, and then I pleaded, "Go on, Granddad, please, finish your story." I felt like a little girl again listening to his tales.

Len Hudson looked at Alex and offered a trifle grin before he continued his narrative of one of the most memorable milestones in his life. The grin faded away as he remembered that he had to kill a man to save his own life. He had to kill his partner. He was twenty-nine at the time, but his partner was in his forties. Len closed his eyes as a single tear rolled down his cheek. In the silent moment in Len Hudson's bedroom, while Alex was staring at her grandfather in the hushed moment, Len stated in a barely audibly sound, an allegation that startled her.

"Please forgive me, Baxter, I didn't mean to kill you, but it was either you or me."

I stood up abruptly, and my chair fell backwards when I heard these words coming from my grandfather's lips. This confession shocked me. *How could this kind, loving man that I've known all my life kill a man, and why?* I thought disconcertingly. I wanted to learn more about this event in my grandfather's life. I couldn't believe what I thought I had heard. There's no way my grandfather would have killed anyone. I bent over and picked up my chair, and then I placed it closer to his bed. I wanted to hear every word that my grandfather was getting ready to disclose. I shook myself off from what I thought was an exaggerated account of my grandfather's tale, and I sat back upon my seat.

My grandfather looked at me, a bit perplexed, but continued on with his life's story. "I'm getting ahead of myself. Please let me continue. Where was I?" He paused to think. "Oh yes, I was living with Aunt Tillie on her little mini farm just outside of Peoria, Illinois. Aunt Tillie had some goats, about a half dozen sheep, and just as many chickens with one rooster, and only one horse. She let me ride her horse all the time. Aunt Tillie also loved to ride, so we'd take turns riding each day since she only had the one horse."

"She was a widow when I moved in with her, but she didn't miss her husband, not like my mother, who missed my dad. No, Aunt Tillie told me many times that her dear deceased husband was a no-good-for-nothing scoundrel, and she was better off without him. She had told me, many times, that if the cops hadn't of killed him, she was getting ready to do the deed herself. She claimed that she was truly grateful to the county sheriffs for setting her free. I got the impression that her dear deceased husband was a dishonest man and mean at that. I learned from Aunt Tillie's stories of Uncle Miller, her deceased husband, that it was a lot wiser and more advantageous to treat people kindly to get respect or to get what you want out of them. All Aunt Tillie ever wanted was a little respect. I guess that's why she and I got along so well—we both respected each other's privacy."

My grandfather diverted from his adventurous tale to offer a bit of description of his appearance and behavior while he lived with Aunt Tillie.

"I was a tall, skinny boy in those days. I didn't start putting on weight until I started to eat the meat from my own hunts, like wild turkey, quail, deer, and sometimes I'd get a huge elk.

I was also a very quiet lad. I didn't talk much. I usually kept my thoughts to myself. I realized that Aunt Tillie and I got along much better when we were both passive and low-keyed with each other's emotions. We got along just great in a quiet din rather than knowing each other's business. Aunt Tillie liked it that way, and I just followed her lead in our living arrangements."

Granddad took a longer pause before he continued with his tale. I waited patiently until he was ready to begin again.

"Aunt Tillie made money selling her homemade goat cheese, fresh eggs, and the wool from her sheep and goats. It was comforting times for me to watch her clean and card the wool each night. She was a good spinner with her yarn from the shearing she'd get from her animals. There wasn't much to do in the evenings on her mini farm. Television wasn't invented yet in those days. I don't think Aunt Tillie would have watched it anyways. We had an old radio, and many times the radio would irritate her, and we would just sit for hours working on spinning and weaving. She taught me how to spin and weave too. I actually got pretty good at it, spinning yarn and weaving, that is. At first, I thought it was only a woman's job, but I got to liking it, and I made some real pretty shawls and some bedroom blankets, but my favorite things to make were horse blankets."

Granddad looked straight into my eyes and tilted his head when he continued his thoughts.

"You know, the kind you put under your saddle to absorb the sweat and cushion the saddle to protect the horse's back. I think Aunt Tillie called them numnahs. Aunt Tillie sold them along with her stuff, and then she would split the sales with me. She used to tell me that since I was producing as much merchandise as she was putting out, and she said that my work was even better quality than hers, that

I should get a partial share of the sales. I sure did like the way she saw things. She always made me feel like a partner on her mini farm."

"I continued to help her for nine years, until I was nineteen. At that time, I remembered reading about some people making it rich in gold mining. I was so enthralled with the West and mining for gold. That's all I could ever think about was gold mining and making it rich. One day, just after Aunt Tillie's sheep shearing fiasco..."

Granddad interrupted his thoughts before he continued his subject of gold mining. He added a tidbit about the hardship of sheep shearing.

"It wasn't as easy as most people think to shear an ornery sheep or a goat."

Len stopped again for a second or two as a huge grin grew upon his face as he reminisced on the events of a shearing day.

"I'm sorry, dear, for the interruption of my thoughts. I did have fun on those days with Aunt Tillie, watching the goats and the sheep jumping around and twisting in our arms. Aunt Tillie and I would laugh so hard each time we saw one of us grab the animal by the neck and get tossed to the ground. It wasn't always hard work without some play. Some of the work was fun. That was my last shearing day with Aunt Tillie. At the end of that day, I had asked Aunt Tillie for some time off to go swimming with some friends."

Granddad stopped again, but this time to really stretch in his bed. I guess it was a bit uncomfortable for him, lying there and relating his story to me, but he went on with his narrative story without any more delay.

"The day after that sheering day with Aunt Tillie, I went swimming in the Illinois River with a bunch of friends, and there I met a man who said that he was going to go West to become a gold miner. He said he just needed a partner, someone to help him dig and pan for gold, and someone to help finance the trip. I volunteered to back him up. I had saved a little over eight hundred dollars in the nine years I lived with my Aunt Tillie. She paid me for my services for helping her in her Homestead Enterprise, that's what she called it, and I saved every penny. I never needed the money I earned for anything, and I never spent any money frivolously. I was eager and overly anxious to give my money to Baxter Bartley. He was thirtytwo years old and had a wife and a newborn son, but he was willing to leave them for a time to try his hand at gold mining."

"I had just turned nineteen, and Aunt Tillie was getting cranky in her old age. I told her about my dream of becoming a gold miner, and she laughed in my face. She said that was the most stupid idea that she had ever heard. That night I left her a note telling her that I was grateful for her kindness, and for taking me in when my parents died. I ended my note by telling her that I would return when I found my gold. About ten years later, I did stop by Aunt Tillie's place to let her know that I found my fortune, but instead, I found that she had died. The neighbors told me she died a lonely woman. I didn't believe them, Aunt Tillie was happy with her animals, and she loved being alone. She tolerated me while I lived with her, and I will always be truly grateful for that, but she was never lonely. Not like my mother, who did die as a lonely woman."

This time Granddad stopped his rendition of his memories to ask for a glass of water. I hustled to the kitchen to gather a pitcher of water and two glasses. My mother stopped me, and asked what I was up to.

"Granddad is telling me one of his tales, and he wanted some water."

"I thought you were going to drive me into town today?" my mother asked, a bit perturbed that I was settling in with her father.

"Gee, Mom, Granddad isn't feeling well today, and he really wants to share one of his tales. You know he hasn't told a story in quite a while, not since he got sick. I feel I should stay and listen to his story. Can't you go by yourself or have Dad take you? I'll stay home and watch Granddad."

I pleaded to stay home so I could hear the rest of Granddad's descriptive history. It was just getting good, and I wanted to hear more about the man that he said he had killed, or I think I had heard my grandfather whisper a confession of the sort. I started doubting what I thought I had heard my grandfather say. I just couldn't believe that my kind, gentle in nature, grandfather could have ever killed a man in cold blood, or in self-defense. Either way, I just couldn't and wouldn't believe it.

Mom agreed to go to town with my father while I stayed home with my grandfather. She hinted that she would probably stay in town with Dad for a late dinner, so I would be alone with my grandfather all day. Then she reminded me of her father's dietary menu. "No spicy foods." I agreed to make dinner for me and for granddad.

Before mom left, I asked her if granddad had ever told her tales about any personal events in his past.

"Hey, Mom, did Granddad ever tell you tales about his personal life?" I asked meekly. I didn't want to divulge granddad's secret of killing a man, not if Granddad hadn't of told her about it.

I had to listen carefully to my mother when she spoke, she has always had a soft, gentle voice. I had to learn, in my younger days, to direct my full attention to her when she spoke, just to hear what she was saying. My mother also kept her feminine girly figure, and she still looks like a rodeo queen with her long, black hair pulled up into a ponytail. My mom always wore country Wrangler's clothes, and she always looked great in her jeans. Her eyes are a deep, royal blue like her mother, my grandmother, and like mine. She is tall and seemingly healthy, and very active on the ranch. I watched my mother stare at me while she contemplated my question.

"No, Dad only told me stories about his adventures. He's always been private about his early life. I've asked him many times to tell me about my grandparents, but he wouldn't talk much about them. He just said that they died when he was young. He did tell me a little bit about Aunt Tillie, but not much more. My dad raised me when my mother died of cancer when I was younger. I was ten when my mother died. Dad did say that was the same age as him when his dad died. I do remember my mother talking about some of their rendezvous before she died. My mom and dad loved to ride together. They taught me how to ride. I guess Dad got that from his Aunt Tillie. I was three when Dad put me on a horse. Even at that age, I could hold onto the reins, and I rode for hours with them. That's one thing we all loved to do together. We rode our horses everywhere. When I got older, in my late teens, I met your father. He looked so fine riding tall upon his steed, and he captured my heart the first moment I met him. After we were married, we moved here to the ranch that your dad inherited from his family, and we've been here ever since."

Mom ended her collective thoughts and turned to leave to go to town. Before she left, she asked me why I was concerned about Granddad's history. I just shrugged my shoulders and brushed off her question.

"No reason," I answered.

I kissed my mother on her cheek as she left with my father, Richard Bush, but everybody calls him Dick. My father is a mellow man, not aggressive, more on the passive side. I never got disciplined by my father, my mother took care of that task whenever she thought that I was being a little overly rambunctious. My father is tall and a little on the heavy side. He stands about two inches over my mother's height which is about five-foot-nine. Dad worked on this ranch ever since he started walking. His parents died a year after I was born and left him the ranch. He has no other relatives except Mom and me.

I stood by the threshold waving goodbye to my parents, daydreaming how lucky I was to have both my mother and my father still alive with me, not like my mother and grandfather who both lost a parent when they were so young. After a moment or two of my idle reverie, I gathered my thoughts, and picked up a tray with the snack plate of cheese and crackers, and the pitcher of water with two glasses, and then I moseyed on back to my grandfather's bedroom. I stood at my grandfather's bedroom door staring at him, and there I saw him lying so still that I thought that he had passed away.

Startled, I called out, "Granddad are you awake?"

"Yep, just resting my eyes, and waiting for my water. What took you so long?"

"Mom was drilling me about what you and I were up to. She's going to Silver City today with Dad. They won't be back until late this evening."

"Good. What I've got to tell you would shock your mother. If you want to tell her my story, when I'm dead and gone, that's up to you. But for now, I'm sharing my story with you."

Granddad stirred uncomfortably in his bed. Awkwardly, he tried to shift his body, and with a painful expression he asked me to help him up.

"I'm tired of being in this bed. Can you help me into that chair? It may take a bit. I'm feeling weak today. No strength in my arms or in my legs. I want to be alert when I tell you where I hid my treasure. It will be up to you to find it, if you want it."

"What's that all about Granddad?" I asked curiously.

"In good time, girl. In good time. Let me continue my story."

Granddad took a long drink of water after he settled into his old worn, but cushy Westgate accent chair and said, "Now where did I leave off?"

"You were telling me that you met a man named Baxter Bartley, and you gave him eight hundred dollars to become his partner to mine gold." I remembered all the details and couldn't wait to hear the rest of the story.

"That's right. Baxter and I left Chicago together. Baxter took my money, and purchased two horses, two mules, and all the equipment and food he thought we needed to survive in the wilderness. The first four years were the worst. We settled in New Mexico where Baxter had heard rumors of gold in the Mogollon Mountains. We backpacked further and further into those mountains for weeks on end, until Baxter finally felt satisfied with the terrain, the topography for mining gold."

Granddad laid his head back onto the headrest of his Westgate chair and fell into a sound sleep.

I stared at granddad as he rested on the overstuffed chair with amazement and awe as to the story I had just witnessed. I pondered on what it would be like to live in the wild of nature without any modern luxuries: sleeping on the ground each night under the moon and the stars, or in the rain, or in any unpredictable weather. *What about food and water?* I thought. These thoughts nagged at me, and I wanted my grandfather to answer my questions.

"Granddad, wake up. You were about to tell me how you survived in the wilderness. Please continue."

My hand was on his shoulder, and I shook him gently to arouse him from his nap.

"Oh, I'm sorry dear. Impromptu naps are a bad habit of old age." He smiled meekly and continued. "Oh, yes, those four years were very gruesome. We almost quit many times because it was so grueling and demanding, but Baxter would start talking about 'when we make it rich,' and his gold bug itch would hit him hard all over again. Each time Baxter moved our campsite, I'd move with him. I just couldn't leave him alone in the wilderness. I knew that he wouldn't have survived alone. He had no survival instincts."

Granddad went straight into his memories and continued his tale. I was excited to hear more without delay. I sat comfortably in the hard oakwood chair directly across from Granddad and propped my feet up onto the bedpost.

"We ran out of food first," he continued with a few stops for a sip of water.

"So, I had to start hunting. I'm not bad at it. I learned a lot of tricks about animals when I was living with Aunt Tillie. She really was a smart old gal. However, she was getting cranky in her old age. I'm glad I left when I did. I heard that she got even meaner when I left. I couldn't write to her from where we were, no post offices in the wild, and we never saw other people for months."

Granddad rattled on about Aunt Tillie for a bit longer before getting back into his tale of survival and gold mining.

"Baxter and I traveled for many full moons before we'd come across any people. Every now and then, we would see another gold miner or a fur trader, but they were far and few. Those four years were very lonely. We'd have gone stir-crazy mad if we hadn't had each other for company. Baxter sometimes got downright batty. He would jump up and start dancing like an old Indian on the warpath. He'd be singing and hollering on the top of his lungs, scaring the birds and the animals right out of their nests or dens. He'd get me to laughing so hard that one time I peed all over myself. Baxter never let me live that one down. He'd tried to top his next crazy spell to make me do it again, but I never did. It was just that one time, but on that one time, Baxter was downright, crazy funny."

He stopped again for another glass of water.

"This storytelling sure does make me thirsty."

I poured another glass of water for him and set it aside on the table next to his chair.

"Here Granddad, so it will be ready for you when you need it."

"Thank you, daughter. That's quite considerate."

"Granddad, how did you survive out there for four years?" I asked.

"Four years." He chuckled. "We were out there for nine and a half years. I just said that the first four years were the worst. After that, things just started to go right by us. We found gold, child. We found gold, and lots of it."

"You found gold! How much?" I asked with an excited grin upon my face.

Granddad just ignored my question and continued to tell his tale.

"Baxter kept moving our campsite to find the right spot to start panning for gold. We traveled into the wilderness for months on end, even years, and finally we came across a healthy flowing stream. Baxter was so tired and frustrated by then. He plopped his whole body in that stream and sat there for a long time, not moving a muscle in his body. He just stared out into the horizon. I watched him carefully for quite some time while I was still on my horse. I wasn't sure if he was going to do something stupid. I could never tell what he was going to do when he got in one of his crazy spells."

"Anyway, I stopped watching him, and I started setting up our campsite. I had just started a fire to make some pine nut tea. We had run out of coffee within the first years of our gold mining quest. Then, out of the blue, Baxter starts screaming. 'HOORAY, HOORAY,' he's yelling. I turned around quickly to see what he was hollering about, and then I saw him holding the biggest golden nugget that I'd had ever seen. The damn thing was bigger than a silver dollar round.

Baxter was doing a jig in the stream where he had been sitting. Then he threw the nugget at me, and said, 'Boy come look at our stream.' I looked straight at him, and his whole face was grinning."

"By that time, I was going on twenty-four years, but Baxter had gotten so used to calling me boy. That's all he'd ever called me. I don't recall him ever using my given Christian name. I stopped what I was doing, and I walked into the water, and right below my feet were golden nuggets everywhere. We just started picking them up. We stayed in that area for three years working a mile or two up and a mile or two down that stream. We ended up with five bags each from that haul alone."

Granddad stopped his narrative and asked me to help him to the bathroom.

"I'm sorry, dear, to have to ask you for assistance, but my legs are still weak. Will you help me up?"

He looked forlorn and helpless when he asked me for assistance. Granddad stretched out his left arm, and I pulled him out of the bulky chair by placing one of my arms around his waist, and then I grabbed his arm that he had held out for me. Once he was up, he wrapped his arm around my shoulder, and we both walked toward the bathroom.

"Are you okay, Granddad? Do you want me to call a doctor, or can I take you to the hospital?" I asked concerned about his health.

"No, I don't want to see a doctor. I think the time is coming close for me to depart this life, but I promise to hang on long enough to finish my story. While I'm in this room, I'd like you to go to my trunk that's in the corner of my bedroom, and up on the top inside lid there's a little pocket on the side panel. Slip your fingers inside that little pocket and pull out the folded paper that I got stored in there, then bring it to me."

I left my grandfather alone to attend to his business in the bathroom, and then I followed his instructions as they were asked of me. I had always been curious about that old, dome-top, steamer trunk with the round bun feet that sat in the corner of his bedroom. Granddad would never let me touch it in my growing years. The trunk had two leather straps with nail head trim. The front had a decorative brass lock and key. I knelt down in front of the treasure chest and slowly opened it. The smell of cedar-wood tantalized my nostrils with the quaint scent of rustic history from my grandfather's past. The right side of the chest had a layered compartment with shelves stacked as high as the rim, and each shelf was filled with mysterious wonder that piqued my curiosity. The left side had a deep trunk space filled with clothing, picture albums, and closed boxes of various sizes. I didn't touch any of his treasures, but my heart wanted to sit there for hours to go through every box, and every shelf to get a feel for all the adventurous stories my grandfather had shared with me throughout my childhood. I dazed into the chest for a moment longer while I heard my grandfather moving in the bathroom. Then I looked up and saw the little pocket with a snap flap on the inside lid. Slowly and as gracefully as I could be, I unsnapped the leather strap on the inside pocket, and then, I placed my fingers inside and pulled out the folded paper that was nestled and snuggled within. The folded paper seemed old and worn as I placed it on the table by the cheese and cracker tray.

"Are you ready to return to your chair, Granddad?" I hollered as I walked back to the bathroom to retrieve him.

We ambled slowly together, back to the stuffed armchair, where Granddad puffed a long sigh as he slipped his brittle body back into his Westgate accent chair. I knew it was the chair that my grandmother had bought him for his last birthday that she had with him before she passed away from cancer. My heart beat harder, and a lump arose in my throat as I watched my grandfather struggle back into the worn-out, overstuffed chair.

Len reflected on hard times when he saw the chair. *Mary, my precious daughter, was only ten at the time my beloved passed away, and I had to raise her alone*, he thought sadly. *She came out pretty good seeing I was doing my best at mothering and fathering at the same time. And here's my baby girl's daughter trying to mother me*, he thought, pleased in his heartwarming reflections as he allowed his granddaughter to lower him into the chair. Then he tried his burliest attempt to get himself comfortable in the seat before he continued his story.

"Alex, did you get that folded paper for me?" he asked, anxious to view his treasure map.

"Sure did, Granddad. It's on the table by the food tray."

I watched my grandfather lean onto the table to pick up his treasure map with his thin frail fingers. He slowly grabbed one corner of the paper and smoothed it out carefully on his lap so not to tear the old, timeworn sheet. The paper had been in that obscure trunk sleeve for over fifty years. There was no reason for him to look at it until now. He hadn't even thought about it in so many years. He had all the money he needed with the ten bags of gold that he brought out for himself when he was twenty-nine. Now he wanted me, his granddaughter, to have the map, to hear his tale, and to eventually retrieve his buried treasure.

Granddad leaned back in the chair to get comfy and cozy to finish his story. "Let me end my life's saga so you can begin yours," he stated firmly with exhaustion.

"When my partner and I panhandled that area thoroughly, Baxter wanted to move upstream even further into the wilderness. I protested persistently each time he wanted to move, and I begged him to return to civilization. I barked at him about his family that he had not seen in over eight years, at that time. His son would have been about seven or eight years old by then. I pleaded with him to go back to his family, to his wife and son, but Baxter always wanted more. He had talked me into settling for ten bags of gold each. He promised me that we would return home after we prospected ten bags of gold for each of us.

"We never did get the full ten bags of gold at that campsite where we first settled. After we prospected one area, we kept moving to another, until we hit it big again. This time, the load was so huge that we ended up with twenty bags each, and another year had passed. I was twenty-nine years old, and I wanted to leave with my gold. Baxter wanted to stay. We verbally fought for several days. I stopped panning for gold when I filled my twentieth bag. I shouted that I had had enough. I'm leaving. I told him. I pleaded with Baxter that our mules and our horses couldn't carry this load, along with our survival gear. I tried to explain to him that we were going to have a difficult time making it back home with the large load that we already had piled on our pack mules and horses. I tried to explain to Baxter that our mules and horses were aging like us, and that they were too old to carry much more."

Granddad stopped abruptly and started coughing in an uncontrollable fit. Blood was in his spit, and he was struggling to get comfortable.

"Granddad, are you alright? Please, let me call an ambulance, or let me take you to the hospital in Silver City." I implored with great concern for my grandfather's health.

"No, they'll stick me on a machine, and I won't be able to finish my story. It's important to me to leave this with you. I don't want those doctors and nurses poking me with needles. I want to give you my legacy, and offer you an adventure, if you choose to accept it."

Len Hudson spit out this last statement in between coughs. He was adamant in his conviction.

I held my grandfather by his shoulders trying to straighten out his body in the chair. I looked into his eyes and said, "Then let me put you back into your bed."

He conceded to the move, and we both struggled to get him back into his bed without more incontinent fits. Finally, granddad's body relaxed in his new position, and he felt more subjugated with his kinetic breathing.

"Alex, please, sit down. I am alright. I want to continue," he said in a soft tone and very relaxed. "I am feeling weak, but I am alright. Please, let me continue. I have a bit more to explain."

I did as I was told but protested my grandfather's lack of concern for his own well-being. I wanted to take him to the hospital, but he pleaded with me to let him die respectfully in his own bed.

"I'm eighty-nine years old, Alex. I am old enough to make my own decisions. Now, please, allow your grandfather his final peace with the world." Len was pleading for his life, the death of his life that is; he wanted to choose his last resting place.

I stared into my grandfather's eyes absorbing all the empathy that he had built throughout his lifetime. I held back tears knowing that my grandfather was dwindling away before my eyes. There was nothing I could do to convince him to go to the hospital, and extend his life, even if it extended it for just a few more days. Those were extra days with me. I love my grandfather immensely. I finally agreed to let him continue his story before I would call for an ambulance.

"Thank you, Alex. I'll settle with that."

I watched my grandfather take another sip of water, then he handed the glass to me. Slowly, he lowered his head to his soft, feathery pillow and continued his tale.

"Baxter and I argued some more when I started to pack up the campsite. I decided to pack everything and force him to leave with me. I still couldn't leave him behind by himself. I felt obligated to watch over him. You see, it was my money that financed the gold mining excursion, and he was my friend, my only companion, for almost ten years. I couldn't leave him alone to die in the wilderness; and I truly believed he would have died alone without my assistance. He couldn't hunt, not like me. He caught a few rabbits at times, but he was never a hunter or a survivalist. I thought that if we started toward home, he would begin talking about how he would spend all his money with his family. I had hoped he would forget about staying, and mining for more gold. It worked for a while."

"We left at the first break of sunrise. I had the animals ready to leave. I had to pack late the evening before, putting his bags of gold on his horse and his mule, and then I had to pack my mule and my horse as well. I worried all night long about our animals. I didn't like the idea that our mules and horses had to carry all that weight all night long, but I was more afraid that I would have problems leaving with Baxter in the morning. It was the only way I knew to keep Baxter to our agreement on leaving at first light."

Granddad dozed off, asleep again, too tired to keep his eyes open. I allowed him to sleep for a few hours. I did not disturb him until it was time for dinner. While he was sleeping, I went to the kitchen to prepare supper for the two of us. I opened a can of chicken noodle soup and stewed a pot of tea. Then I made two grilled cheese sandwiches, one for each of us. Just as I walked into my grandfather's bedroom with the tray holding our meal, Granddad awoke in a foul mood.

"Don't let me sleep like that again until my story is done," he snapped angrily at me.

"Well, I had to make supper, and I'm starving. It was the perfect time to leave you alone while I did the cooking." I snapped right back at him. I did inherit some of his stubbornness. I caught my grandfather smiling as I placed the tray of food on top of his bureau. I could see his reflection in the bureau mirror.

We finished eating in silence. Neither of us said a word throughout our meal. I picked up the empty bowls and left the teapot and cups. I hustled the dishes to the sink in the kitchen as I left Granddad alone looking at the map that I had retrieved earlier.

"I'm ready to continue my story, thank you for the soup and sandwich. It was delicious, and I guess I was hungry after all." He stated apologetically as I returned from the kitchen.

"Yeah, it was good." I agreed with the tasty meal and asked my grandfather to continue by reminding him where he had left off.

"You ended your story, before dinner, by telling me that you packed all the mules and the horses with your gold and with Baxter's gold, and then you started to return home."

"Yes, Baxter followed in a numbing stupor. He was cranky and belligerent. He followed because he didn't want me leaving with his gold. We traveled for several weeks without too much trouble, but as time wore on, Baxter was getting even crankier and even more belligerent. He kept shouting obscene, profane smut at me. And I do mean, vulgar, nasty shit. I had to tie his hands to his saddle and gag his mouth. I couldn't handle hearing him. I took the restraint and gag off when we settled at a campsite for the evening, but each day after about an hour of his verbal abuse, I had to tie him and gag him again until we settled for another night. I did this for several weeks. Finally, he stopped talking all together, so I didn't have to gag him anymore. We traveled steadily for another week, but then he started acting strange.

"We proceeded for days on end in a calamitous, off-and-on, haggling. It was turning out to be a long and slow process toward society. Baxter's mood was changing rather drastically. He stopped helping me altogether with chores at our campsite, and with the horses and mules. I was becoming overly tired, and his constant nagging was draining me fast. To make matters worse, it had started to rain. At one of the stops for the night, there was a quick summer mountain cloudburst. It was annoying to ride in. We ended up under a mountain ridge that had a steep hallow overhang near a flowing riverbed. I stopped to observe the exquisite terrain that we had just passed near a forest timberline. I decided to settle there for our evening camp. The region was beautiful. There was a mixture of bushy Mesquite and Piñon trees in the meadow below the ridge. The ridge itself hung over a stream that was flowing from the rainfall. The forest scent was mesmerizing with the smell of damp Piñon nuts. I had gathered some Piñon nuts that had fallen to the ground and roasted them on a campfire just before settling in for the evening.

"That night, I laid under the stars trying to get some sleep, but Baxter was stirring restlessly in his sleeping gear, and each time he moved, I jarred awake. I was so tired the next morning from lack of sleep. I didn't want to move on until I got more rest. Baxter was acting extremely eerie by then, and I had to watch his every move. I was afraid that he wanted to harm me. He would constantly stare at me. I could feel imaginary daggers up my spine. I was so tired with watching Baxter and not getting enough sleep, and my intuition was nagging at me to keep a closer eye on him.

"We were running low on food again. I had to leave Baxter alone while I went hunting. He promised me he would settle quietly until I returned with my hunted game. I knew he was hungry, so I didn't worry too much about leaving him on his own. I filled the animal's water bags and our canteens from the flowing stream before I left. I put Baxter's canteen by his sleeping gear. Baxter was still in his bedroll sleeping when I left early that morning to hunt for some game.

"It was a little over eight hours before I was able to return with my catch of several small animals. I didn't want to leave Baxter alone for too long. I did catch up on some sleep while I was gone. I took a short catnap as I nestled my body under a tree while I was waiting for some wild game to pass by. It worked, for I felt refreshed. The short rest, and mostly being free from Baxter's creepy disposition was exhilarating.

"As I slowly trotted into camp while still on my horse, I noticed Baxter was fidgeting by his horse and the mules. He was acting strangely, but he seemed to be interested in my every move. He had a shovel in his hand, and I saw that he was perspiring excessively. I asked him what he was doing, but he wouldn't answer me. He just started to walk off into the mesa, away from our bivouac.

"WHERE ARE YOU GOING? WHAT ARE YOU UP TO? I shouted at him as I dismounted from my horse and laid the game across a rock.

"He turned and offered a baneful smile that gave me a quiver down my spine. I followed him to a hole he had dug in my absence. I stepped slowly toward the aperture that he had dug that was four feet deep and about three and a half feet wide. It wasn't a perfect symmetrical niche. It was more spherical with large rocks protruding from the perimeter.

"Baxter stood behind me with the shovel still in his grip. His hands were turning white with the tight pressure he had as he clenched his fists that were wrapped around the shovel handle. As I looked down into the hole, I saw twenty bags of gold tossed into the pit. Fear jabbed me instantly as I realized that my bags of gold were being buried in a hole that was also meant to be a grave for me.

"I turned quickly with fear with a lump in my throat when Baxter lunged toward me with the shovel held high above my head. Baxter swung the spade cusp directly toward my forehead. I jumped to the side, sliding on some loose dirt. I turned quickly as I tried to maintain my balance. Forcefully, I pushed Baxter away from me, shoving him hard with both hands. It was a survival instinct. Baxter lost his balance, and he fell into the hole, hitting his head on one of the rocks that protruded from the peripheral wall of the hole that he had dug earlier for me, to rest in peace for all eternity.

"The shovel tumbled down and hit me on the top of my crown. Blood was dripping from my head and running between my eyes down past my nose. I wiped the blood with my sleeve, and then I vigilantly turned to reason with Baxter. But Baxter was dead. He lay twisted in the grave that was meant for me."

My grandfather looked at me with tears in his eyes. He cried for several minutes, undisturbed by me. I just sat there gazing at him, not knowing what to say, or what to do. I watched my grandfather reach for a tissue to wipe his eyes before he stopped crying. I walked over to his dresser, and I poured a fresh glass of water. I handed the glass to him while my hands were shaking.

After granddad took some water, he stared into my eyes and I stared back, but with softer more compassionate eyes. I moved closer to him and stretched out my hand to reach for him in his bed. I pulled myself in closer to my grandfather, and then I gave him a long, emphatic, loving hug.

"It was an accident, Granddad, just like you said earlier. You were defending yourself. Baxter Bartley swung the shovel at you, to kill you. It was either you or him. That's what you had whispered earlier." I defended my grandfather's actions, but I believe that my grandfather thought differently.

"Yes, it was an accident, but I knew he had gold fever. I should have done more to help him through his crazy stages."

"Granddad, what more could you have done? You only pushed him away so the shovel wouldn't hit you. What did you do after you saw that your partner was dead?"

"I pulled Baxter's body out of the hole and tied him over my mule. I transported his body back to his wife and child. But before I left, I filled the hole that Baxter had dug for my grave, and I left the twenty bags of gold still in it. That's what this map is for. I had a compass, and I was able to mark and survey the area from the mountain ridge where we camped. This particular ridge has a deep hallow ledge that overlooks a dry bed. I'm sure that dry bed is full and rapid after a mountain thunderstorm, but I believe it drains and dries quickly. There is a large boulder that is propped up against nature's suspended wall, just under the overhang. The overhang protects the boulder from inclement weather. Before I returned to civilization by myself with Baxter's body draped over my mule, I carved an epitaph on that boulder, like a gravestone for the memory of Baxter Bartley.

"Here's where Baxter Bartley departed this land. A gold miner, husband, father, and friend.

"The gold is buried fifty-seven steps to the south of that boulder. This map will direct you to the treasure that I left in that hole."

Granddad struggled to lift his body to hand me the map, then he continued to say, "The gold is yours, if you want it." He let go of the map as I grabbed it, and then he plopped back down onto his bed. He closed his eyes and fell into a deep, disturbed, sleep.

I left granddad alone for several hours to rest and sat in the kitchen sipping a cup of coffee. I had to ponder and think about this most captivating story that I had ever heard. My thoughts were heavy. *Should I take the challenge and try to find the buried treasure? I'll have to talk to Mom and Dad about this and see what they want to do. I know that Granddad is giving me this quest, but it belongs to Mom, not just me.* I was absorbed with deep concentration in my thoughts. Then, I remembered that Granddad had mentioned that there were forty bags of gold between the two partners. *Twenty bags were left behind in the hole where Baxter died, and then he said that he kept only ten bags. What did he do with the other ten bags of gold?* I thought while I sipped my coffee.

I walked back to my grandfather's bedroom and watched him sleep restlessly in his bed. I could see that he was agitated in his sleep, and I felt that he just might awaken soon in his disquieted slumber. I just sat there staring at him until he had awakened on his own. I waited patiently, watching my grandfather in his bed, my mind still wandering, still heavy with concern if I should take his quest. I wanted to know about the other ten bags of gold, but I had to wait until Granddad awoke from his exhaustive sleep to find out about this question that intrigued me.

I worried about him. He was moving feverishly, and his breathing became more sporadic. Suddenly, he awoke in a coughing sputter.

I rushed to his side and threw a robe over his slumped shoulders. I pulled him out of his bed, and practically dragged him to my new Ford pickup truck. He didn't really struggle with me. He seemed to be in and out of a cognitive state. I shoved his body onto the front passenger seat of my new truck, and then, I drove him to the nearest hospital some sixty miles away.

I knew that I could get my grandfather to the hospital much quicker than an ambulance. The nearest ambulance service was in Silver City, an-hour-and-ten-minute drive from my parents' ranch. I contemplated the ambulance's trek and realized that the ambulance would have to turn around and make the same trip back to Silver City for the nearest hospital. I could eliminate half of the transporting time by taking him to Silver City myself. That was exactly what I was going to do. I strapped the passenger seat belt around my grandfather and tried to get him as comfortable as possible, but also as secure as possible at the same time. Cautiously, I drove to Silver City at nine-thirty at night. I turned the radio off; I didn't want to hear the assiduous noise from the radio. I only wanted to hear Granddad's breathing.

Please don't die, Granddad, I thought. Those dire and daunting words kept screaming in my mind as I continued the forlorn jaunt to the Gila Regional Medical Center in Silver City.

Chapter

TWO

Dick Bush's cell phone rang three times before his wife, answered it. "Hello," Mary said.

"Hey, Mom, I'm on my way to the Gila Regional Medical Center in Silver City. Granddad is coughing up blood, and he's much worse than he has been for weeks. I'll meet you and Dad at the hospital." I hung up before Mom had a chance to say a word. I knew she would be upset with me for not giving her more information, but I didn't want to get into any discussions with her, especially while I was going to be driving at night, in the dark. I was under enough stress.

The Gila Regional is a full-service hospital in Catron County, and the only hospital in a-hundred-and fifty-mile radius in the southwest region of New Mexico. I had grabbed two bottles of water to take with me on our trip to the big city. I also clutched my granddad's pillow to try to make the trek a little more comfortable for the long ride as I hustled him out the door.

Granddad was too weak to argue with me. He allowed me to manipulate him to do my bidding, and I wasn't in the mood for any haggling. I got pretty scared when I observed his erratic breathing, and I sensed that something was wrong with him. All I could think of was to get him to the nearest hospital.

My grandfather slept most of the way there while I drove just a little over the speed limit.

I was anxious to get him to the hospital, but I knew that speeding would only add a few minutes to my destination. I wanted us both to get there safely. I set the auto speed control to seventy-eight miles per hour and drove diligently on Highway 180. My thoughts rambled on while I drove in silence, grateful for the emptiness of other automobiles on the desolate mountain road. The radio was off to keep it quiet while Granddad slept. Every now and then, I would stretch my right arm to reach for my grandfather's robe that kept slipping to the floor. I had to lean to the right and grab the end of his robe to drape it over him. I tried tucking and driving at the same time for several miles. I finally gave up the 'tuck and drive' maneuver when his robe fell for the third time to the floor.

Granddad awoke bewildered by his environment. It took him a few minutes to realize that he was in my truck. His head was dripping with sweat, and his temperature was rising with fever.

"Alex, do you have the map?" he questioned me nervously. He wasn't sure how long he could hang on to life. He was so tired, so very tired and weak.

"Yes, Granddad, I left the map at home. It's too frail to keep folding and unfolding. I must get a copy made and preserve the original. Why, what's the problem?"

"No problem. I just wanted to be sure you could read the map and find the buried treasure." His voice became weaker. I could hear his energy draining from him quickly as he struggled to catch his breath.

I slowly stepped on the brakes to release the auto speed control. As I lowered the speed of my truck, I began a conversation with my grandfather for the rest of the trip to the hospital. I wanted him to feel at ease while he gathered his composure.

"How are you feeling, Granddad?"

"I'm all right. It's my time, and I don't think I can hold on much longer. Please don't fret child. I want to go. It is my time. You know your grandmother has been waiting for me, and I don't want to upset her. She has been waiting a very long time for me. She's a good woman. I've missed her so much in these long years without her. You look a lot like her. Did Mary ever tell you that? That you look a lot like her mother."

Len Hudson stopped talking and looked long and lovingly at his granddaughter, who was trying to pay close attention to her driving and to her grandfather who was slipping away from life just a few inches from where she sat behind a steering wheel.

I tried to hold back my tears, but it wasn't working. Giant waterdrops started gushing down my cheeks, and my eyes were burning with the salty water from my tears. I slowed my driving speed again, and I concentrated on the road, but a lump began to swell in my throat. I had to stop. My left hand gripped the stirring wheel tightly, and then I directed the F-150 to the side of the highway. Slowly, I lowered the speed to a stalled stop. Immediately, I burst into tears, unable to control my emotions.

"Granddad, please, stop talking like that. We're only a few miles from the hospital. I can have you there within fifteen minutes." I reached for a tissue from the glove compartment and blew hard and dewy until my emotions were in harness. All of a sudden, I felt ashamed of myself for crying. This was unbecoming of me. I had always conducted myself in a hoyden fashion, especially since I knew that my grandfather always wanted a son or grandson. This girly behavior with tears and emotions was just going to upset him, and that was the last thing I wanted to do in his final moments in life.

"Alexandria."

He called me by my female name instead of the male nickname, Alex.

His voice was soft and languid, "I am very proud of you. You are a beautiful woman, like your mother and her mother before her. You do not have to find the gold if you don't want this adventure. There is plenty of money in my account that you and your mother will inherit. Each bag of gold is roughly worth about three hundred and fifty thousand dollars, and I only used five or maybe six bags out of my ten that I brought out of the Mogollon Mountains. I've liquidated all the remaining bags and deposited the money in the bank. You can always get the buried gold years from now, or you can bequeath the quest to your child or grandchild. It doesn't matter. I don't want you to feel pressured in doing this quest that I'm offering you."

Len shifted his weight to look directly at Alexandria and took in a deep breath of air before continuing his soliloquy. "What is important to know is that I truly love you, you and your mother. I know I've treated you both like one of the cowboys on the ranch, but I didn't have that feminine touch that young ladies need. I guess, I raised Mary to be manlier in some respects, and she reared you in the same manner. I believe. No! I know that I can rest peacefully knowing that you both can take care of yourselves without relying on any other person. This truly makes me happy."

I sat in my truck, behind the steering wheel, still and solemn, staring at my grandfather. He had closed his eyes to rest after that long speech. He had become weaker, and his breath was very shallow. I pulled myself together, and started the motor up again, then quickly, I revved the truck onto the highway to continue toward the hospital. Within twelve minutes from where I had stopped earlier, I was pulling into the ambulance emergency entrance at the Gila Regional Medical Center. I ran into the emergency room and begged for assistance.

"I NEED HELP, PLEASE. I NEED HELP NOW," I shouted.

A nurse rushed to my side and followed me to my truck. She grabbed a wheelchair by the sliding door and pushed it as we hustled toward my vehicle. She opened the door and grabbed my grandfather's wrist to feel for a pulse. I stood back and observed the large woman take control of my grandfather as she pulled him out of the truck. She shoved him into the wheelchair, and then she rushed him into the hospital. One-half hour later I was sitting in the waiting room with my mother and father while Len Hudson was being probed with needles by the attending nurses who doted over him.

Four hours had passed, and the admitting nurse had completed her paperwork. She had informed us that we would find Mr. Len Hudson on the second floor in room 217, where he had been placed to peacefully die. It wasn't a private room but a semiprivate room for two occupants. The other bed had another elderly gentleman who was dying from lung cancer. There were several people sitting around the bed in the other occupancy. Mary drew the curtain fully around her father's bed to give her father some privacy.

Len had informed the hospital staff that he did not want to be connected to any machines that would extend his life. Since he was coherent and within his facilities, the hospital administration had to comply with his wishes. Mary and Alex both ran to Len's bedside when they saw him connected to only an IV drip. I understood this setup and tried to explain it to my mother.

"It's Granddad's dying wish, Mom. He didn't want to be on any machines. He had told me earlier at home that he did not want to be hooked up to any machines to extend his life. He wanted to die at home, but I couldn't leave him at home while he was in pain. I had to take him here to the hospital, but he did insist that we should not extend his life with machines. He wants to be with your mother. Please Mom, let's honor his dying wish." I stared at my mother and watched her nod her head in agreement, while tears were gushing down both her cheeks.

"Now, now girls, I'm not dead yet." Len opened his eyes and offered a cool composed grin and winked at Alex.

"Oh, Dad, I'm sorry for crying. I promise to be strong for you." Mary sniffled and wiped her eyes, and instantly changed to a dominant, controlled caretaker.

"Alex, have you told your parents about our conversation today?" Len asked, now wide eyed, alert, and full of pain-releasing drugs.

"No, not yet I thought I would tell them this evening when we were all together at home." I reported.

"Mary, Dick, do you mind if I continue my story with Alex alone for just a bit longer? She'll explain it to you later." Len composed a grin to ease Mary's fears.

Dick grabbed Mary's purse while Mary gave her father a kiss on his cheek before leaving the room. Mary nodded to Alex and whispered, "I'll see you in a little bit."

Len reached for Mary's hand before she left, and stared directly into her eyes and said, "Mary, my sweet daughter. You have provided me with many pleasurable hours of pride and love. I truly hope that you know how much I love you. I am very proud of you.

"Now, if you don't mind, I need to continue a story that I was telling Alexandria before she rushed me here to the hospital. She'll explain it to you later. Thank you, Mary. I love you."

Mary lowered her head and kissed her father one last time before she left the room with Dick. Then she nodded her head toward Alex as Alexandria shrugged her shoulders.

I watched my mother and father leave my grandfather's hospital room, then I grabbed the hospital room bedside chair and leaned in closer toward granddad so that I could hear his aging, weak voice.

"As I was trying to tell you on the way here in your truck, you don't have to take on this quest to find the gold. But if you do, will you do me a favor?" Len stared into her eyes, afraid to look away to miss her answer.

I widened my eyes with interest. *What could be so important to Granddad that he would request a favor on his dying bed,* I thought, intrigued but emotionally drained.

"What can I do for you, Granddad?" I whispered as I leaned in close to him.

"If you accept the quest and take the adventure to find the gold, you will find twenty bags buried according to the map. The favor I ask is to give ten of those bags to Baxter Bartley's living relatives. Baxter's wife's name was Laura, but I believe she died a few years after I returned Baxter's body. His son's name is Buster Bartley. I think he was about the age of twelve or fourteen when his mother died. He should be in his sixties by now. The last time I saw them was when I brought in Baxter's body to be buried with his family in Chicago, Illinois, some fifty years ago."

Len stopped to catch his breath but hustled to continue. He felt drained, and he wasn't sure he would be able to finish his request before he died.

"You might have to find him. Get a detective to help you, if you can't find them on your own. Maybe Baxter's son, Buster, got married and had a family? Half of that gold belongs to Baxter and his family. I feel obligated to give it to Baxter's family. Can you understand?"

Len waited for Alex to agree or disagree. He felt guilty all these years for killing Baxter. He knew that it was self-defense, and all he did was shove Baxter away to protect himself from the shovel that Baxter tried to hit him with. He had told the authorities, when he brought Baxter's dead body back to town, that Baxter died by slipping on a rock. The authorities did an autopsy on Baxter and found grit, rock slivers and dirt in the wound. He was pronounced dead by accident. The police did not question Len's story, and Len did not tell all the gruesome truth.

I watched my grandfather; he hadn't moved an inch since his last question. "Sure Granddad, I can understand. That's what you did with the other ten bags of gold. I was wondering what happened with the other ten bags that you brought back with you. Now I understand.

"When you were telling me your story, you had mentioned that there were twenty bags of gold for each of you, but you only kept ten bags for yourself, and twenty was left in the hole where Baxter died. I was wondering what happened to the other ten bags. I believe you gave the other ten bags to Laura and Buster Bartley years ago when you brought back Baxter's body. Am I right, Granddad?"

"Yes, I gave ten bags to Laura many years ago. Buster was only nine years old at the time. Ten of those bags are still Baxter's, and his family should have them." Len looked at his granddaughter with loving respect.

"Okay, I promise that if I take your quest, I will give ten bags of gold to Buster Bartley or to his remaining family." Alex smiled at her grandfather as her royal blue eyes sparkled by the light on his bed.

Len Hudson was at peace, and he could now die free of all obligations that tormented him for over fifty years. He could never go back to retrieve the gold himself, not with the memories of his friend's death. The death of his friend by his own hands, even if it were in selfdefense. Len Hudson felt relieved that someday the indebtedness would be fulfilled, and his guilt would be absolved.

Len laid his head peacefully on the soft feathered pillow that Alex had clutched from her grandfather's bedroom before she drove him to the hospital.

Len closed his eyes, and whispered in a faint expiring voice, "Thank you, Alexandria."

I watched my grandfather's life fade from his body. I couldn't feel a pulse on his wrist, and I feared the results. I rushed to the door of his hospital room, and then I hollered for a nurse.

I stood in the corner watching the doctor and nurses try to revive Granddad without any success. My mother came running into the room when she heard my scream for assistance. My dad quietly walked over to his girls and hugged us both, until we both stopped crying, which was for a very long time.

Chapter
THREE

Alex and Mary both walked over to the hospital bed, and they stared at Len Hudson.

Mary grieved softly, and leaned over her father's body, still in shock of his sudden death. *Alex just brought him to the hospital;* she thought in her grief as she continued to cry. She gently kissed her father's cheek while holding back more tears that welled up in her mournful royal blue eyes. She turned toward her daughter and asked her what her father had said to her on his dying bed.

"Granddad had told me a story today about his younger days when he lived with Aunt Tillie and when he was a prospector for gold in the Mogollon Mountains. He gave me a map where he buried some gold. Then he asked me to give ten bags to his deceased partner's family, if I choose to go find his buried treasure."

I didn't offer to share the part where my grandfather had said he had killed his partner. I decided that I would let my grandfather take his secret with him into his departed life. That bit of information would be a secret shared between just me and my grandfather's memories. I swore to myself that I would never tell another person about his secret. I felt that if he had not spoken to anyone in all these years about that incident, then it wasn't up to me to share it either.

Mary stared at Alex and questioned her about her father's tale, "He told you about Aunt Tillie and his younger years? He's never mentioned his early life to me. Why would he share his memories with you and not with me?"

Mary was jealous of her daughter's closeness to her father, especially now, on his dying bed. Mary's thoughts were wandering. *I've always been a good daughter. We were so close, Dad and I, since mother died. I can't understand why he would tell Alex about Aunt Tillie and his prospecting days, and not tell me.* Mary snapped out of her thoughts when Alex spoke up.

"Gee, Mom, I don't know, maybe he thought that since you married Daddy, you weren't interested in his quest for his gold."

"But he never asked me, if I was interested."

"He told me that he had mentioned it to you when you were my age, but you eloped with Dad and got pregnant with me. What can I say, Mom. I don't know why he shared it with me, but he was really concerned about his old partner's family getting ten bags of gold."

"How many bags of gold are left?" Mary asked indignantly, still bewildered as to why her father chose to tell his granddaughter about his prospective days and not his own daughter.

"He said there are twenty bags that he left behind buried in a hole near a ridge with a deep hallowed ledge that overlooks a dry bed. He gave me a map and said that I could find his hidden treasure by following his map. I left the map on his bureau in his bedroom. The map is old and frail, and it needs to be copied before it disintegrates."

I was physically tired, and emotionally exhausted as well. I didn't want to argue with mother about granddad's tale, so I turned around and started to walk out of the hospital room, leaving my mother and father alone with my deceased grandfather.

"WHERE ARE YOU GOING, MISSY?" My mother hollered at me in a rude, annoyed tone.

I turned around and walked back into my grandfather's hospital room. I marched in front of my mother and stared directly at her for several silent minutes, eye to eye, and then I questioned her, "Why are you doing this, Mother? I don't understand you. Why are you angry at me?"

"You're right, Alex. I'm acting the fool. I'm sorry. I guess I'm in shock. I just…" Mary paused to catch a tear that was beginning to welt in her already puffy royal blue eyes, and then she continued. "I just can't believe that Dad's gone. He's truly gone. It was only Dad and me for so many years. Then I met your father, and I got pregnant right away, and you came along. Then it was the four of us—you, me, Dad, and Granddad. I've never been away from him. Dad has always been in my life. He even moved into your father's family home when your dad's parents passed away. Dad said that he wanted to help us with the ranch since I wasn't able to help your dad because I had to take care of you."

My mother was rattling on. Her voice rose an octave, and she began to talk faster. My father stepped forward and told us both that he was going to reserve two hotel rooms and that we were all going to stay in town for the evening.

"I'll go back to the ranch in the morning to take care of the animals while you two remain in town and make the arrangements for Len's funeral."

We all agreed to stay in town for the night. It was too late to drive back to the ranch, and arrangements did need to be made. We were all too emotionally drained, and physically too tired to drive safely for another hour and a half back to the ranch in Glenwood.

We gathered that evening in my mother's and father's room at the hotel. I heard my father call one of our ranch hands, and asked him to secure the stalls for the evening, and to lock up the chickens in their coop. This was done each night for the safety of the chickens since there were so many wild cats, coyotes, wolves, and raccoons throughout the Apache and the Gila Wilderness that tended to be scavengers late in the night. We've lost several chickens in the past that way before, but not since my father started locking them up in their coop each night. The wild foragers could not break through the chicken wire coops, and the wild scavengers were shot at when they hunted during the day.

Dick swallowed hard after he gave his ranch hand his last orders; now he had to inform them of Len's death. Len was liked by all the cowboys on the ranch, for he was one of them. Len would rise early each morning, seven days of the week, and offered to help the cowboys with their duties. He was always one of the cowboys, sharing stories, chewing tobacco, and doing chores.

My mom and I heard my dad clear his voice before sharing the sad news to the ranch hands, and this sparked another lump in our throats. When Mom began to cry again, I joined in, and we both cried until we fell asleep. I slept with Mom that night and Dad had my room to himself.

PART TWO

THE QUEST: RETRIEVING THE GOLD

Chapter

FOUR

The quest began. It all started when Dick Bush asked his daughter what she wanted to do with her grandfather's legacy.

"Hey, Baby, now that your Granddad's funeral is over and your mother and you just finished writing your last thank-you sympathy cards, are you going to find Len's buried treasure?"

Dick looked directly into Alexandria's eyes when he spoke. His wife and his daughter both have the same spellbinding royal blue eyes that seemed to mesmerize him every time he stared into them. This was the attraction that caught his heart when he courted her mother, Mary. Mary was a beautiful country girl. She was Rodeo Queen for Catron County at the age of nineteen and she held that position for several years. The County residents could never find anyone qualified enough to take the crown away from her, not until she was in her midtwenties. Even then, she was still a beauty, smart and ambitious, but her ambition was for a family life. Mary felt that she was too old to be county queen, especially since she had an infant daughter to her charms.

Infant daughter, now look at her. She's my pride and joy, Dick thought. *And she's as beautiful and smart as her mother. I can't believe that her mother would choose me as her beau with all those other young, handsome cowboys chasing after her. I sure was the lucky one to capture her heart.* Dick smiled at his daughter as he continued his pleasant thoughts of his life with his wife and daughter.

"I'm calling my sorority sisters this afternoon, Dad. I don't want to do this quest on my own. I want to offer the quest to my three dorm roommates. They're my closest friends. I'm sure they'll come. I'm a sister in distress. Right?" I jested playfully, but my thoughts were more adverse. *They'll come, but they won't stay after they hear my request,* I thought.

I was worried that my friends wouldn't want to go with me on my treasure hunt on the long, arduous trip. I continued my thoughts; *it would be a rather long trek into the Mogollon Mountains with just the bare necessities of life carried on the back of a horse. I'll bring pack mules to carry small tents, sleeping bags, food, clothing, and water, but my friends are more city girls than cowgirls, like me. I'm not really sure they will be able to hold up on this expedition.* My thoughts were more concerned for their safety, *but I don't want to take this trip alone.* I continued my thoughts while I stared blankly at my father.

Both Dick and Alex were deep into their own thoughts when Alex interrupted with a comment about calling her sorority sisters.

"I should call them right away and get this over with." Alexandria stated uncertainly. "I'm going to offer each person that comes with me a bag of gold for their support and effort. What do you think about that, Dad?"

"Didn't you talk to your mother about that already?" Dick asked. "I thought she said she would do whatever you decided on your grandfather's request."

"Ya, she did. I just wanted to hear your point of view."

"Well, I really don't feel that I should have a say on how you plan to use the money or the bags of gold. However, if you do go on this trek, then everyone who plans on going with you must heed to my directions."

"Absolutely, Dad. I wasn't questioning that. I just wanted to know how you felt about the entire trip?"

I was trying hard to get dad's feelings about the whole endeavor, especially about offering a bag of gold to each of my friends. I was also frightened for the safety of my friends. I knew that they were all city slickers and didn't have a clue as to what they were going to get themselves into with the long haul into some very rigorous terrain.

"Whatever you decide to do, I'll back you up. If you plan on going to find Len's buried treasure, then I'll lead the expedition. There's no way I'm going to let you and your friends loose in the Mogollon Mountains." Dick was done with this conversation and retreated to the kitchen.

Later that afternoon, I called three of my college girlfriends and asked them to bring their boyfriends to my father's ranch. I called each one of my sorority sisters individually to offer the invitation. I had one left to call, and I had to beg her just like I did with the other two sorority sisters.

"Please come Suzanne. I have a proposition to offer you and your boyfriend, Rick. I've called Brenda and her boyfriend Brian, and they said they wouldn't miss it. Lizza is also coming. She just broke up with Wayne and doesn't want him involved. It sounded like a bad breakup."

I had heard that Lizza found Wayne with another girl from our sorority. I'm not sure who was the cheating sorority sister, and I didn't ask Lizza to convey that bit of information. I knew it would hurt Lizza to mention the Bitch's name, and I also had other things on my mind at that moment. I thought that maybe this proposition that I had suggested to her just might be what Lizza needed to get over her cheating boyfriend. I directed my thoughts back to Suzanne and waited for her to say something.

"What's this all about?" Suzanne asked.

"I don't want to get into it on the phone. Please let me know if you're interested. If you show up on Saturday, then I guess you're interested. If you don't, that's okay. I'll tell you all about it at another time, after we get back. Talk to you later. I've got to go."

I cut my conversation short with each of my sorority sisters that I spoke with. I didn't want to answer questions. I only wanted to offer the proposition once to the entire group, and not have to explain it a dozen times.

My mother prepared a garden party, a barbecue, for all my guests. My father was cleaning the back yard and was staying out of the way of the women. Earlier that day, I had locked myself in my bedroom preparing a statement to read to everyone that would be present to hear my proposition. I wanted all three of my closest girlfriends to go with me on my quest, and I thought that they would all enjoy the adventure if their boyfriends also came along. However, my greatest concern was that I honored my grandfather's last request on his dying bed.

My thoughts of my deceased grandfather kept haunting me. *I just lost the best friend I ever had. Granddad has always been there for me, all during my growing years, he was a huge attribute in my life. He was my best friend.*

I was unable to continue writing my proposal. In the solitude of my bedroom, I felt sad and depressed. I had to stop writing several times because I kept thinking about my grandfather.

A tear rolled down my right cheek, and slowly I lifted my arm to wipe it away with my blouse sleeve. My thoughts were back on my grandfather's funeral that was only a week ago. I sniffled in instead of getting a Kleenex.

I miss you so much, Granddad. I thought as I held my head while I leaned over my desk to try again on my proposal. I stumbled on the draft that I was writing. *Granddad said that there were still twenty bags of gold buried in the Mogollon Mountains. He wanted ten bags to be given to his old partner Baxter Bartley's living relatives. If my friends all come with me on the quest, I can give each one a bag of gold. Let me think, there's Suzanne and Rick, Brenda and Brian, my boyfriend, Effram, and Lizza who is single. Poor girl, catching that SOB with another girl from our sorority. That will leave four bags left for Dad, Mom and me. I know my friends can use the money to pay off their college tuition. Mom and Dad can use theirs to renovate the ranch. Then there's another ten bags for Mr. Bartley's family. I'll have to find his family when we get back.*

I fell asleep at my desk as I finished writing my statement to convince my friends to take this long, and possibly burdensome, camping trek into some of the most rugged terrain in the southwestern mountains of New Mexico.

I awoke when I heard my mother banging on my bedroom door. "Alex, get out here. Your friends are starting to arrive."

"SORRY MOM, I FELL ASLEEP AT MY DESK," I shouted to her through the closed door. "I'll be right there." I stated in an intentionally softer voice.

I jumped up and ran to the bathroom and splashed my face with cold water. *It begins, and there's no turning back.* I thought as I continued to throw water on my face.

The mirror in the bathroom reflected my image as I looked up at myself. I stared directly into my own eyes. *I can see why Dad gets so captivated when he stares into my eyes, or Mom's eyes,* I thought as I turned my head toward the door. My grandfather was always making remarks about my eyes. He would tell me every day about how attractive my eyes were, and how he thought that God gave you those eyes to confuse the devil. One day my father heard my grandfather tell me that phrase, and he started to say it too. I got used to hearing that expression from both my dad and granddad.

I was purposely going slow in my bedroom, hoping that time would give me some courage. I had jitters in the pit of my stomach. I was afraid that my friends would not want to take my grandfather's quest with me. I really wanted to do this for granddad, but heaven forbid, I did not want to do it alone.

Everyone waved at me as I walked down the stairs to the front parlor of my parents' home. Effram, my boyfriend came over and gave me a hug and a fervent kiss in front of everyone there. My mother gasped and choked in a loud guttural throat clearing. She had never seen me kiss my boyfriend before. Actually, she just recently met Effram for the first time only a week earlier when he attended my grandfather's funeral.

The second-year semester had just ended, and I wanted to invite Effram to the ranch to meet my parents, but granddad had died before I could invite him to meet my parents more formally. Effram and I got really close this past semester where he had told me he loved me on several occasions.

My father was a little more relaxed about the situation than my mother. My father walked up behind Effram and lightly squeezed his shoulders before he quietly whispered to him, "You may want to hold back some of that passion you have for my daughter, at least until her mother and I can get used to it."

"I'm…, I'm sorry, sir," Effram said apologetically with a stutter, "I hadn't seen her in over a week, and I sure missed her." Effram said while clearing his throat.

I blushed when Effram grabbed my hand and squeezed it. My father put me at ease when he winked at me, but my mother was still fuming and turning red while she stood near my sorority sisters. I dropped Effram's hand and walked over to my mother and grabbed her arm. I whispered to her, "Can we talk *later* about my relationship with Effram? I want to get this proposal over with. My stomach can't take much more of this anxiety, and I am eager to see if they will all come with me on Granddad's quest."

"All right, but we *WILL* talk this evening," she said to me as she turned to sit in the recliner in the corner of the den. Her face was softening a little, but I knew that I had a lot of explaining to do later, after everyone left or went to their rooms for the night. We lived a long way from the University dorm, so my parents offered everyone a place to sleep for the night. My parents were modern in the social scene, but they refused to have the couples sleep together in their home. My mother didn't have time to clear my grandfather's bedroom. There was only one spare bedroom available, and Suzanne insisted that she and Brenda should share that room. If Lizza stayed the night, then I was going to share my bedroom with her. Effram, Brian and Rick would all have to share the den.

I stayed standing by the fireplace and asked everyone to find a seat. I watched each person pick their spot in the den. This amused me to watch them gather while they were all in their own reality.

Suzanne Leyba, who was the more authoritative of all my sorority sisters, took the first seat. She grabbed the most comfortable seat in the room. Her boyfriend, Rick, grabbed a dining room chair and placed it next to hers. Suzanne was a pretty girl with light brown hair and light brown eyes. She had a narrow Roman nose and carried herself with dignity. Her family worked in the banking industry, and she was reared to express herself almost as royalty. She did act in this fashion, but she was never snobbish about it. She just had high standards in her pride. I met her parents several times in the past two years, and I understood why Suzanne had to act this way. Her parents insisted that her academic grades must be above normal, but her social life had to also reflect in this same high standard. I knew that this had put a lot of pressure on Suzanne, and she always seemed to push harder than everyone else. Her parents' expectations of her always seemed to be her most important reason for everything she did. She was the one person I thought who would turn me down first.

Rick Buffano, Suzanne's boyfriend, was the athlete of the bunch. He was on the college football team. Of course, he was built like a football player, tall, husky and aggressive in his mannerism. His face was wide with a few scars from earlier tackles during some offense or defense moves, while on the football field. He played rough and received rough—this made him a true asset for his team. He would do anything Suzanne told him. He wasn't one to think on his own, and Suzanne was one to order people around. They were the perfect match. He loved Suzanne and felt proud to be with a girl with her high standards, and she needed a boyfriend whom she could boss around. I knew that if I could get Suzanne on my side, then Rick would follow, no matter what.

Brenda Garcia was our down-to-earth girl. She chose to sit on the floor near the fireplace, close to me. She wore her dark brown, curly hair short. She liked her hair short; it was easier to keep clean and brushed. Since her hair was very curly, it tangled a lot. Keeping it short made it much easier for her to keep it looking combed. Her eyes were hazel on the greenish side. Brenda's quirky nature gave her the appearance of a friendly sprite. She laughed all the time. Everything seemed to amuse her. This was a great feature in her, for she always kept our group in stitches, even on our gloomiest of days.

Brenda had a bit of a weight problem. She was pleasantly plump, but not overly obese. She exercised every day to try to keep her weight in balance, but she did love her parents' food chain. Her parents owned all eight of the hamburger franchises in Las Cruces, New Mexico. Brenda's parents were always asking to buy out their competitors.

They wanted to be the only family-owned hamburger franchises in Las Cruces. Brenda and her siblings were to inherit all eight of their parent's restaurants, but it was Brenda's business prowess that kept all eight in Las Cruces financially successful.

Brenda's boyfriend, Brian, was just her opposite. He was much taller and thinner than her. He wouldn't eat red meat at all; however, he was hooked on chicken sandwiches, and as long as he dated Brenda, he could have all the chicken sandwiches and French fries he could eat for free. Brian sat on the floor with Brenda. He scooted himself right behind Brenda to give her support to rest her back while she sat on the floor. Brian was like that, always thinking of Brenda.

Brian Sebastian White comes from a lower-income family. He is working his way through college. He studies hard and works even harder. He'll take any odd jobs that are offered to him. If he can get money for the job, he'll do it, no matter how messy the job can be. He can't work a normal steady job because of his studies. He's working on being an electrical engineer, and he must work hard to keep his grades up. If even one class is under a B grade, he'll lose his scholarship. He can't take the chance of losing it. He doesn't have enough money to support himself without that scholarship. I wasn't worried about him accepting the offer to my proposal. I know he'll take it even if Brenda refuses to come.

Next, I watched Lizza Hernandez. She waited until everyone was seated before she grabbed a chair far off toward the back of the room. She was gloomy these days since she caught her boyfriend with another woman. She hadn't had enough time to get over the bum. Yeah, that's how I felt about her ex. He was an SOB, a rotten bum, and I know that all my sorority sisters felt the same way about her ex, except for the one bitch that slept with him. I felt sorry for that sorority sister, for I heard that she was going to get a humiliating expulsion from our sorority. Poor Lizza, she looked pretty pathetic in her sad, droopy face. I'll have to push her to come along with us. I believed that this trek was what she needed to get over that bum.

Normally, Lizza is a beautiful girl. Even more attractive than Suzanne. She has nice facial features, smooth skin, suntan in color that keep the boys interested in her. She wears her long blond hair just past her shoulders. And I can tell you that she looks great in a bikini with her slim waist and her large bosom. I don't think she'll refuse the proposal. I think she's just waiting for something to get her out of her stupor. I never understood why her ex-boyfriend cheated on her. Lizza was the most beautiful woman in our sorority. She was the most beautiful woman at the state university. Lizza's reputation was sincere by all our sorority sisters as being the most friendly, helpful and generous person anywhere. She was liked by everyone. Since gossip flew quickly at the dorms, everyone considered her ex a foolish moron, for no one understood why anyone would cheat on the most beautiful catch at school. I actually felt sorry for her ex as well. Now her ex was stuck with the cheating sorority sister who was soon to be ousted by the entire sorority house.

After I checked out my sorority sisters and their mates, I directed my attention toward Effram Towsend, my boyfriend. My father had placed two dining room chairs together and directed Effram to sit in one of them, and then my father sat on the other side of him. Effram was staring at me and nodding for help, but I couldn't rescue him from my father. I had to let him sit there for the rest of the day until I finished with the main purpose of the gathering of all my friends.

I met Effram at my sorority house Halloween party. One of the senior girls had invited the male fraternity to come to our Halloween party. At that time, Effram was a freshman like me, and was dressed as Robin Hood. The costume that I wore was a bit more seductive. I wore a fairy princess outfit. I was a bit more alluring as an enchantress elfin. I wore a low-cut black bathing suit, black tights, some glitter on my face and on my outfit, and a pair of sparkly wings. Effram had entered the sorority house from the main entrance, and I entered from the rear of the house; we both headed toward the kitchen. I was carrying two bags of ice, one in each hand. I had just been ordered to fetch more ice by my seniors. When I turned the corner a little too quickly as I entered the kitchen, I ran right smack into Effram. One of the bags of ice slipped from my hand and split open and dumped on his lap. Instead of the ice numbing his private parts, he ended up with a huge erection. To make matters even worse, I had fallen directly on top of him with my legs spread wide over his lap. His erection was quite distinctive in his Robin Hood leotards. My costume became a tremendous success that night. I had won the grand prize for the best costume. Effram's fraternity and my sorority both voted my costume as the best costume to create an arousal. How could I turn Effram down when he asked me for a date? Especially, after I embarrassed him in front of his fraternity. We've been together ever since that Halloween night.

I stared at my boyfriend, Effram, for a moment or two. He wasn't the best-looking man in the room, but he sure was the most charming. He stood at medium height around five-foot-ten and weighed about 140 pounds. His eyes were deep brown, and his hair was of similar color. His love of life and all of nature around him is what made him a beautiful person. Effram was levelheaded with strong beliefs in Christianity. His study was related to youth ministry. His parents were missionaries who traveled to third world countries, helping with education, social justice, health care, and of course, spiritual relief.

Effram was working for a bachelor's degree in theology. He wanted to be a Big Brother minister to help develop spiritual growth in the younger teens. I thought it was interesting that he got to delve into subjects related to metaphysical and religious philosophies and doctrines. Our evenings together were composed of debates on religious issues instead of sexual contact. Oh, don't misunderstand this, Effram loved to make out as much as I did, but he never tried to get to third base. We kissed a lot and had some exciting moments, but Effram would never disrespect me to push for anything more until I was ready, or until he was ready. I didn't think that Effram would turn down my quest, but his studies were very important to him. So, he was iffy in my mind.

My mother stood up and addressed everyone there, "Hello everyone. I would like to thank all of you for coming to hear Alex's proposal. Does anyone want any refreshments before she gets started? I will bring out some glasses of punch in a while. Please, Alex, would you start your meeting while I go to the kitchen and get the barbecue ready for everyone when you are done." After my mother's little speech, she turned and walked out of the room, leaving everyone else staring at me.

"Thanks, Mom," I mumbled. My face started to get red. I was put on the spot. It was my turn to speak. I opened my mouth, but no words came out. I took a couple of deep breaths and stared at my father.

My father did not get up and leave the room like my mother did. He continued to stay seated right next to Effram. I looked at him and watched him nod his head like he was telling me to move on without words, just body language.

"Oh...Okay, I guess it's time I told you all why I gathered you here today." I spoke slowly and a bit nervously. "As you all know, my grandfather recently died."

I stopped and caught my breath and inhaled deeply again before I continued. I could hear my friends offer condolences in low dolor voices.

"Well, Granddad had told me a story before he died. He said that he had buried twenty bags of gold in the Mogollon Mountains. He had left me a map with directions on where to find these twenty bags of gold. I have asked you here to invite you all to come with me to find this buried treasure. For your assistance in this arduous trek, I am offering you one bag of gold for your help. I believe, according to my grandfather's account, one bag of gold is equal to about three hundred and fifty thousand dollars, maybe a little more in today's market." I stopped my rendition of my grandfather's quest to watch their expression to the invite of a new adventure.

Their response wasn't what I had hoped for.

At first, I heard gasps for the enormous amount of money that each bag could be worth. I assured them that Granddad had informed me that each bag held enough gold pieces to equal that amount of money. And that I was giving them each one bag for their support in my quest.

Brenda questioned first, "You want us to hike into the Mogollon Mountains to hunt for gold? Are you INSANE? Do I look like Annie Oakley?"

I stood there dumbfounded. I didn't expect that kind of reaction. I had hoped that they would be a little more enthusiastic about the invitation of an adventure. "I will supply the horses, mules, and all the supplies for the trek," I volunteered, talking a little faster.

I was surprised to hear from Lizza next. Lizza talked slowly and with a very soft, meek voice, "How long do you think this adventure will take? Do you think it will be difficult?"

"I'm not really sure. I studied my grandfather's map, and I am estimating that the entire trek, there and back, should only take about two weeks. My grandfather had told me, before he died, that they, Granddad and his partner, Mr. Bartley, had traveled for several weeks before he had to bury the gold. We won't have to travel into the deep wilderness to find the gold. But the trek will still be somewhat difficult."

"I don't know if I can handle it," Lizza said with a quivering voice. She was still in selfdenial and humiliation from the breakup with her boyfriend, Wayne.

"Come on Lizza." I pleaded. I really wanted Lizza to come on the quest. I truly believed that the trip would help her heal. "You'll be in my tent with me, just like our dorm. I'll help you with everything. I really think this quest is just what you need to get over that bum."

Lizza nodded her head in approval without any words. I think she was holding back tears when I called her ex a bum.

Suzanne was next, "Two weeks?" She questioned. "Two weeks, but we'll miss the beginning of our next semester. That starts in exactly one week from tomorrow. How can we ever get back in time for school?"

"I've already talked to Dean Moray at the New Mexico State University, and I gave him a heads-up to my quest that my grandfather had bequeathed to me. He was quite excited for us to have an opportunity like this. He said that he would love to come himself, if he were younger and did not have the college to contend with.

He offered an approval for two weeks of absence until our return to school for the next semester. He gave us his approval to continue onto my grandfather's quest. Dean Moray even offered to get each of us a tutor to help us catch up with the other students when we returned after the quest."

Brian was all for it. All he heard was that he would get a bag of gold worth 350,000 dollars or more for just camping in the wilderness. "NOT A PROBLEM FOR ME. I LOVE CAMPING," Brian shouted boisterously with a grin.

"Thank you, Brian. I'm grateful to have your company on this trek." I said pleased to have one person accept without hesitation.

"Just wait one cotton-picking minute," my friend Brenda sneered. "You're not going anywhere without me, Brian; and I'm not sure that I want to play Annie Oakley for two weeks. I've never been on a horse before. To tell you the truth, I'm afraid of horses. I'm afraid to get bucked off. I don't think that I would fall very gracefully." Brenda did not look happy with Brian's enthusiasm to be a member of my expedition.

Brian smiled at his girlfriend and stated, "Don't worry baby, I'll teach you. I've ridden horses many times. Last summer I worked at McGregor's riding stables. I got to exercise every horse that old man McGregor had in those stalls, and exercise for a horse is to ride a horse. I've ridden many different horses." Brenda returned the smile to Brian, and shrugged her shoulders before she replied, "Are you sure about this? Do you think that I could do this without falling?"

"Sure, you can, Brenda. There were kids of all ages at that riding stable, and every one of them learned to ride like a true cowboy and cowgirl. I don't see you having any problems learning to ride." Brian offered with encouragement. He really wanted to go on this trek. He wanted a bag of gold worth 350,000 dollars, or more.

"Well, okay Alex, I guess you can count on Brian and me to go with you." Brenda said with a quiver of uncertainty in her voice.

"Thanks Brenda, and you too, Brian." I smiled at the two of them and turned to look at the rest of my friends who were staring at me.

"Effram, I haven't heard from you yet. Will you go with me?" I paused and waited for him to answer. I wasn't positive that he would go with us, just because he was my boyfriend. I knew that he wanted to continue with his studies, that was more important to him than anything else. Even the bag of gold was not a temptation for him. I thought of an idea that might persuade him, so I blurted out my thoughts.

"Effram, you could bring some of your books to continue your studies on the trek. Plus, we would need someone to keep a prayer vigil over our adventure." That did it. He was hooked. I knew he would say yes when I looked into his eyes. He would want to protect me, and who better to keep a prayer vigil over this diversified bunch than a student of theology.

"Okay, Alex, I'm in," Effram answered. "This could be a great experience for me to keep us safe through prayer."

Suzanne stood up and Rick followed her movements. I thought that she was going to leave, but she paced the living room floor for a few steps, back and forth, back and forth. She seemed to be in deep thought. Rick stood by her like a bodyguard watching her every move. Everyone was quiet until she stopped pacing and turned to address us all. Suzanne always spoke like an official representative, and straightened out her posture and then declared, "Okay. Rick and I will go, if Dean Moray gave you his word that it was okay for us to miss a few weeks into our next semester. My parents will have a freaking breakdown if I mess up my college education. I've got to graduate with HIGH honors."

I nodded my head and quickly said, "Oh, yes, Dean Moray gave me a written permission slip for all of us. I have given Dean Moray all your names, just in case you all said yes to accompany me on my quest. It even has an added idiom about giving us tutors to help us catch up with the rest of the classmates who started before us."

I waited for a response but didn't get anything verbally. However, they all started to mumble amongst each other.

I quickly interrupted their meandering to show my appreciation to everyone present. "Thank you, everyone. I am truly grateful to have you all come with me on this adventure. Granddad said it should be a great learning experience for me and for all of you."

My father, who just sat there the entire morning, finally stood up and addressed us all.

"Alexandria, are you sure you want to go through with this crazy quest that your grandfather baited you into?"

"Yes, Dad, I'm sure."

"I thought so. I knew nothing would stop you, especially when Len induced you with one of his tales."

"That's not fair, Dad. Granddad did not entice me with his tale. I really want to do this."

My father asked, "Why do you want to do this?"

"Well, I guess you're right, Dad. I do want to fulfill Granddad's final request."

"Well enough. Your mother and I thought you would want to continue this quest. She asked me to speak for her today. She cannot come along with you. She knows that it was her father's dying request, but someone must stay behind to run the ranch. And as you know, your mother is not the adventurous type, so I will be going with you on this quest. Your mother and I had talked about this extensively, and we already prepared everything for you. There is a horse for each of you in the barn. We will pack six mules with all the tools, tents, food and necessities that we should need for this adventure. We will leave in four days. That should give you all plenty of time to return to your homes or dorms and retrieve your personal items that you plan on bringing with you, like your books, clothing, and whatever you want to bring. Just remember that you must pack your personal items on your horse, and maybe you could find some room on one of the pack mules. The pack mules will carry all our living essentials. Please remember, all of you, to call your parents and let them know that you will be going on this quest with Alex. You are all 21 or older, and do not need your parents' permission; however, they should know that you will be gone from school for two weeks. I will leave you now to discuss this amongst yourselves. Please, don't make Alex's mother wait too long to serve her delicious barbecue." Dad got up and left the room, like he always did when he felt he was done with a conversation.

We all talked for another half hour and then hurried to the kitchen for the banquet that my mother prepared for us. We were all starving. The aroma had been filtering through the living room all morning.

My friends departed directly after lunch. No one wanted to spend the night because they all wanted to get ready for the quest. It would take them one day to return home, a few days to prepare, and the last day to return to my parents' ranch. And then, we would be on our way the very next day.

My mother grabbed my hand and pulled me into the den where we could talk alone, after I said my last goodbye to everyone. Mom sat first and directed me toward the opposite seat.

"Now tell me, how serious is this relationship between you and Effram?" my mother asked questionably.

"Mom, you don't have to worry. Effram is a decent man, and he won't do anything to hurt me. We haven't had sex, if that's what's bothering you." I stopped and coyly smiled at my mother.

I'm twenty-one years old, and old enough to live my own life the way I please, I thought, before I said my next sarcastic remark. "Not yet anyway."

Mom did not like my added quip and snapped back at me. "Well, maybe I am curious about your relationship. I just don't want you to get pregnant before you graduate from college. Can you understand that?"

"Of course, I can understand that Mother," I said defensively, using the proper noun for Mom. "Effram is studying to become a minister, and he is fighting the temptation of his emotions and desires against his faith and doing the right thing. You see, mother, it was me who wanted to have sex with him, but he turned me down. To tell you the truth, that just turned me on even more."

I turned my head away from my mother. We've never had an argument like this before, and I was a bit embarrassed to discuss my sexual feelings with my mother. I guess she must have understood the way I was feeling, because she gently picked up my hand and patted it lovingly.

I turned my head in her direction and continued. "I fell in love with Effram, Mother, and I know he loves me. He tells me all the time. Now, I am the one who is trying to keep him faithful to his religion and his beliefs. I believe he is grateful to me because I stopped the pressure of offering myself to him. He hasn't asked me to marry him yet, but I think it's coming. Sometimes when we're kissing, he gets excited, and I can feel his arousal. He thinks he can hide it from me when he stands up quickly and walks away."

Mother smiled at my last comment, and then added, "Maybe you're right. A man can only hold back for a short while. I believe the sex drive in men is much more vibrant than in women." She held her breath for a moment and stared into Alex's royal blue eyes with her royal blue eyes and stated, "Well, usually the men have stronger urges, but my daughter can always prove me wrong. Who knew that you would have the stronger urges?" We both laughed, and we hugged each other. Then she smiled at me before she offered her approval of Effram as a son-in-law. "I think Effram is a good man, and if you love him, then, I will love him too."

Mother stood up after our talk. I also stood up and hugged her with loving intent from deep in my heart. I knew she felt the love for me just as much, for when she hugged me back, she held me tight for a long time before she let me go.

We both left the den quietly together, and walked directly toward the kitchen to clean up the huge mess that was left from the barbecue lunch.

Chapter
FIVE

Tuesday morning arrived rather quickly for me, and I'm pretty sure it felt that way for everyone else. I purposely awoke early to be ready when my friends arrived to begin my quest. I slowly stretched out my arms and then I raised them to the ceiling. When I lowered them, my whole body shook with a shudder. I thought about my sorority sisters. They were much more than just sorority sisters; they were my true friends. I was grateful to have such wonderful friends, friends who would attempt this bizarre adventure for my sake, and others who were probably coming not just for my sake, but for 350,000 dollars. The only one who really wanted to go was Brian because he needed the money; the others were skittish about the adventure. Some of them have never been on a horse before.

Oh yes, I thought to myself, *this is going to be a bizarre adventure for them, and also for Dad and me.*

I heard commotion outside my bedroom door. This was my clue that Mom and Dad were already up and about. I could hear Mom preparing a large breakfast for all our guests. She was busy puttering around, but she didn't look happy. I think Mom was dreading our trek. Dad was coming with us and leaving Mom to do all the chores on the ranch alone. She wasn't going to be totally alone. Mom and Dad had hired two ranch hands that have been working for us for several years. They were trustworthy men, and they both had families, wives, and kids who stayed in their own cabin quarters on the ranch. Their kids actually liked living on the ranch. They got to ride our horses as often as they wanted. It worked well both ways for the ranch hands and for us. When the kids went riding, they exercised our horses. To keep a ranch horse trained, they should be ridden at least twice a week or daily if possible. Mom sure couldn't do that chore alone with all the horses we had and with as many horses that we bordered.

"Good morning, Mom," I said as I walked into the kitchen.

"Good morning, dear," she replied. "Alex, may I talk with you before your friends arrive."

"Sure, Mom."

"I don't mean to put a damper on your quest, but I have to give you this warning that I had in my dream last night."

Mom looked even more forlorn now that she was sitting by my side. She grabbed my hand and held it for a few quiet seconds before she continued.

"I had a disturbing dream last night. It was very frightening. I feel that something terrible is going to happen on your trip. I know that I can't stop you from going. You're as stubborn as your grandfather ever was, but I want you to be aware at all times. Watch over your friends. They are new at country life, and they do not know the dangers of the wilderness."

"Oh, Mom, I think you are putting too much dread into this. We'll be fine. Dad is coming with us, and my friends are adults. They can take care of themselves."

"Yes, you're right," Mom said, "I think I am putting too much dread into this, as you said. But please, always be watchful."

Mom brushed my hand one last time and kissed me on the cheek, and then turned to continue her cooking by the stove. What perfect timing to end our mother-and-daughter freaky talk. Just as Mom got up, I heard several vehicles pulling up simultaneously. I ran to the front door to greet my friends. I saw Dad walking toward the corral and wave to everyone as they drove in.

Dad had directed each one of my friends who drove a vehicle to park it in the barn. We were going to be gone for two weeks, and Dad did not want all the vehicles left out in the weather elements for all that time. The automobiles would also be in the way of every day feeding and caring for the livestock.

The ranch hands had spoken to Dad earlier when they were told of my adventure. They had sworn to Dad that they would take good care of Mrs. Bush, my mother, in his absence. Dad offered to give them a good bonus for their true diligence on his return.

Everyone was in high spirits. The adrenaline was hitting each member of my quest. Brian had put Brenda on a horse for riding lessons the moment they arrived. Brenda was a bit perturbed because Brian would not let up on her and would not let her go to breakfast with the rest of the consortium.

I had started thinking of our group as a consortium, like a business group that was in a financial venture together. When I offered to give each member of my team a bag of gold for their participation, I turned my quest into a business venture. So, a consortium we have become.

Brenda and Brian finally settled in the kitchen for their breakfast, just as the rest of us were finishing up. Dick Bush pushed his chair back and walked over to a blackboard that was resting behind some kitchen towels.

"Glad you could make it to breakfast," Mr. Bush announced to Brenda and Brian. "Please eat and listen at the same time as I must go over some criterion before we depart tomorrow morning at sunrise."

Dad deliberately looked at each one of us at the table before he continued. There was total silence at the table. Dad continued, "I have been studying Alex's map that her grandfather had given to her for this gold expedition. We will leave from here at first light tomorrow morning. My ranch hands will help to saddle your horses and help mount our gear onto the six mules that will be carrying our survival equipment into the Gila Wilderness. I'm estimating that it should take us less than a week to reach the mountain ridge where Len had buried the bags of gold, a day or two to dig it up and relax before we return home. I figure it should take us only a week and a half, or possibly two full weeks to complete Alexandria's quest. That accounts for any bad weather that we may come across."

The room started buzzing with the murmurs from my consortium. Lizza was the only one quiet. She came alone without a mate and felt like an outsider. Rick, Suzanne's boyfriend, the husky football player, was reaching for another pancake that was left on the platter. Suzanne handed him the plate with the leftover bacon. Brenda and Brian were both grabbing for their food before Rick claimed his seconds or was it his third or fourth helpings. I was pointing at the blackboard and whispering to Effram. Everyone was talking to someone else other than listening to my father.

Dad walked over to the table and slammed both his hands on the edge. Everyone was startled and jolted. They all looked up. Even my mother, who was still cooking at the stove, stopped and stared at my father. I had jumped as well and stopped talking to Effram and stared at my father.

Dick firmly stated, "Now hear me well. I need your full attention. This is not a ride at an amusement park. This trek is a long and possibly dangerous journey. We will be riding our horses every day for hours. Your butts will be sore, your thoughts will wander, and your strength will weaken as we journey forward to our destination. We will be traveling in some rugged terrain with loose rocks that are slippery for your horses, and there is cacti that have very fine pointed needles. If you fall, it will hurt. It will be hot, dry, and at times, if the weather changes, it will be wet and muddy. If you do not pay attention to me, you will not survive. Alex was born into this region and has a feel for this type of environment, but city slickers, novice riders such as yourselves, will not enjoy your first few days. I am trying to prepare you so that you can endure this journey."

"I'm sorry," was echoed throughout the room by everyone there.

"Thank you. I will continue. As you can see on this blackboard, I have drawn a small map that resembles Alex's map. We will ride all day tomorrow, and for the next few days until you are all feeling like one with your steeds. Your horse is your survival. Treat that horse with love and kindness. Your horse is your responsibility. You will feed it each night, and you will give it water each day. You will brush your horse each night and before you place your saddle upon his back. If your horse gets saddle sores because you are not caring for it properly, then you will walk the next day so your horse can heal and recuperate. Believe me, you don't want that to happen."

Brenda interrupted with a quivering voice, "I told you, Alex, that I've never been on a horse before."

Brian jumped in, "That's not true. You were riding this morning, and you were doing very well."

Brenda blushed with her boyfriend's praise, but she knew that she was not an Annie Oakley. Brenda still feared her horse.

"I'll help you with your horse each night," I offered to calm Brenda. I could see the fear of the trek overcoming her, and we hadn't even started. Brian volunteered to help her too.

Brenda was feeling a bit embarrassed by being the center of attention that she nervously set upon herself. "Thank you, Alex, and you too Brian. I'll take you both up on that offer." She smiled a small smirk and stuffed a bite of pancakes into her mouth.

When breakfast was over, they all gathered in the living room of the Bushes home. Each one was preparing their private bedroll that Mr. Bush had just finished explaining to them on how to keep their sleeping gear clean and dry, and ready to go at any time of the day. Dick had also given each member of the team their own saddle bags that would carry their personal items that they chose to bring on the journey with them.

The day just seemed to be over. Mother made a light dinner for us. We were all mulling around talking about our horses and our gear when my father spoke up.

"Well, is everyone ready? We've got to get started early tomorrow so that we can get at least fifteen to twenty miles under our belts." Mr. Bush said. "It's off to bed with all of you. Mrs. Bush will wake you up early tomorrow morning, and she will cook your last homemade meal before we all leave. The men will sleep on the floor with your sleeping gear that was handed to you earlier. The girls will sleep upstairs, also in your sleeping gear that you received earlier. I want you all to get familiar with your gear."

"I'm ready Dad," stated Alex.

"Me too, sir," said Effram.

"Okay, from here on, NO one will call me SIR. My name is Dick. You all have my permission to call me Dick. I'd much rather be called by my name then to be addressed as sir each time you want to talk to me." Dick stopped and looked at each one in the room.

"Sure thing, Dick," I said.

"Let me correct myself. All except you, Alex. You still have to call me, Dad." Dick said with a grin upon his face.

Alex's consortium all laughed as they grabbed their sleeping gear and scattered to their assigned sleeping arrangements.

Morning came too quickly for everyone. Mrs. Bush was cleaning up after the huge breakfast. Everyone offered thanks to Mary for the great food that was waiting for them. The consortium all left together toward the barn to help the ranch hands, who in turn were setting up the mule train for their departure.

"Mr. Bush." The foreman of the ranch hands approached him.

"Yes, Randy." Mr. Bush addressed his foreman as he walked toward him.

"Are you all ready to leave? We have packed all your gear as you requested."

The ranch hand followed Mr. Bush past each animal and explained to everyone what each mule was packing. Mr. Bush directed each member of the team to a horse that was assigned to them.

Dick continued his training to Alex's coeds and showed them how to place their manta, their horse blanket, upon their horse making sure there was nothing that would rub up against the manta and the horse's hide, before the saddle was placed over the blanket. He continued by teaching them how and where to place their saddle bags and their sleeping role. They were shown how to tighten the cinch on the harness under the belly of their horse, where to safely place the bit so it won't cut their horse's mouth, and finally, how to place the reins around the horn of their saddle.

Another hour passed before they all had properly saddled up and were ready to mount their steeds. Alex was in the house with her mother saying goodbye, since she had been riding since she was three years old. Alex did not need the extra training that Mr. Bush was giving to her consortium.

"Mom, we're leaving now. There will be no way to reach you on our trek. No cell phone service out in the wilderness."

"I know dear. I will wish you and your father good night, every night, before I go to bed. If something goes wrong, I know I will sense it, but you are on your own out there. Please remember my warning. I feel it so strongly. Please watch over your friends." Mary kissed her daughter and followed her to the stables where everyone was waiting.

Dick walked toward Mary and grabbed her like a movie star and kissed her passionately. Everyone, even Alex, whistled and hooted as they watched Mary blush when Dick walked away and mounted his steed.

Before the consortium started to move out on the dirt road that exited the Bush Ranch, Effram asked to offer a prayer for their safety on their trek. Effram directed everyone to lower their heads in respect as he prayed for the safety of the entire group, even for the safety for those who were staying behind to manage the ranch without Mr. Bush's assistance.

"Amen." They all said together when Effram was finished with his prayer.

As soon as the last word was said, everyone began talking simultaneously. High spirits were felt by all as they slowly marched out rather impetuously upon their steeds. Mary and the ranch hands were waving goodbye along with the ranch hand families.

Mary lingered to watch her family leave until she couldn't see them anymore. She held her stomach for a pit of pain stabbed at her as she tried to push the forlorn thoughts that weighed heavily on her mind. She couldn't brush off the fear of the thoughts that something dreadful was about to happen to Alex's consortium on this quest that was requested by her father on his dying bed.

Mary bowed her head and said a prayer to protect her family and her daughter's friends. "Please Lord, watch over them. They are greenhorns and need your protection. I fear that the devil will be following them with harmful intentions. Please protect them all."

Mary took a deep breath and walked back toward the main house. She had tons of chores to do before night fall.

Chapter

SIX

The first day was rough for everyone; even Alex and Dick had a troubled day. Brenda whined all day, only when she was on her horse, which irritated both Dick and Alex. Brenda was only happy when they all stopped for a rest. She was totally different when she was dismounted from her horse. She would crack jokes and make everyone laugh at the silliest of incidents. When she tried to remount, Brian had to help Brenda up on her horse each time she attempted to boost herself up. She just couldn't get a handle on the stirrups. Brenda was always the last person to be ready to leave, except for Brian who had to give her a final push each time she mounted her horse. It seemed that Brenda had two left feet. For some reason, when Brenda put her left foot into the stirrup, she couldn't lift her chunky body up onto the saddle and then swing her right leg over the saddle to place her right foot into the stirrup.

On one occasion, Brenda mounted herself backwards and was facing the horse's tail. Brian would not allow her friends to laugh at her. He did everything he could to help her out and make her ride on her horse more comfortable. Brian didn't seem to mind giving her the boost each time she had to climb upon her horse. He loved Brenda. He truly loved his chunky girl. Brian truly believed that Brenda's dyslexia was created by her abnormal fear of horses. Actually, Brian was very proud of his precious dumpling for her persistent effort to control her fear so that he could be on this expedition with her friends. She knew how much he needed this extra money for his tuition. Her family had worked hard for their money, and Brenda knew the value of her family's money. She was very proud of Brian for his diligence in his studies and work habits to succeed. Nothing was ever given to her either. She also had to work hard for her money. This mutual attitude toward hard work and success was what made their relationship so compatible. They were a perfect couple together.

Brian's family did not understand the infatuation that he had with Brenda. Brian was handsome, a gentleman, smart, and witty. Many gorgeous women sought after Brian's attention. There were many times while Brian and Brenda were on a date together at a local restaurant, an attractive woman would interrupt their date to offer Brian her personal telephone number and blatantly ask Brian to call her. These bold and arrogant women would do this in front of Brenda as though she were just a piece of furniture at the table. Brenda would just smile at them and say, "He's my lover, bitch. Get lost." Brian just loved it when she did that to the contemptuous beauties. The women would look at Brenda then back at Brian, as Brian would raise both his hands and shrug his shoulders, then he would nod his head in approval and blow a kiss toward Brenda. Brenda would pretend to grab his kiss and smear it upon her lips. The women would act offended and hustle away from their table, embarrassed.

Brenda was a lovely woman in her own right. She was just a little heavier all around. Brian loved his chunky girl. He had dated several pretty women in college, but every one of them cheated on him and went with the richer man because he refused to spend his hardearned money on them. Brian was not born into a wealthy family. He had to earn every penny to make ends meet. And college tuition was an extremely high expense for him. Dating those pretty woman was even more exasperating for him, for they always wanted so much attention. It wasn't just physical attention, they also wanted expensive trinkets as gifts from him to show his love toward his beautiful date. The last woman he dated before he met Brenda, was a cheerleader for the college football team. She was so spoiled that he did not even enjoy the sex that she so freely offered to him. All she cared for was being seen at the most expensive restaurants, wearing the most outrageous outfits, and receiving the best gift of all the other cheerleaders in her squad. Brian couldn't keep up with her expensive desires.

Then he met Brenda. She came from a wealthy family. Her parents owned eight hamburger restaurants in Las Cruces. Brenda was not spoiled. She had several brothers and sisters whom she had to compete with in her family. All her siblings had to work at one of the restaurants to show support to the family business. Brenda had to earn her college tuition by working at every family restaurant that her parents owned. She was successful in every one of them. It was Brenda's intellect that caught Brian's attention in the first place. Brian had frequented almost every hamburger restaurant in Las Cruces and noticed Brenda in many of them. Then he met Brenda in one of his classes at the university. Brian was smitten at first sight. This was a woman who loved everything he loved. She had to work hard to earn a living, even though her parents were wealthy. He believed that she would never cheat on him and date another guy while she was dating him. He asked her out several times before she would accept. She thought that he was making fun of her, but Brian persisted and convinced her that he was sincere, and they have been best friends and lovers ever since. Brian also found out that Brenda was the best lover he had ever been with, a wild cat under the sheets.

Mr. Bush was grateful that the first day for the consortium was stressful but uneventful. The course through the wilderness was right on track according to Len Hudson's map. Dick had taken control of the copied map; the original was too old and worn to carry. He felt that Alex had her hands full keeping her consortium content, especially with Brenda, when she whined while on her horse. The rest of the team seemed to block Brenda out. They all had their own demons to conquer while riding all day in the hot sun with saddle-sore butts.

Suzanne's ride was the most pleasant of all Alex's friends. Rick was always by her side. At one time, Rick reached over and picked up Suzanne's hand and then blew kisses at her. Suzanne pretended to grab for those kisses and acted like one got away, and then she pouted like she felt sad that his kiss missed her lips. Rick leaned in and kissed her affectionately to reassure his love to his queen of the female equestrians. Suzanne was on a natural high; she was away from her overbearing, dominant parents. She was able to live freely in her own thoughts and her own actions. She enjoyed these feelings that were so unreal, and these rich emotions were hers alone, not emotions due to her authoritative parent's rule. These were emotions that she could cherish forever and not have to share with her controlling parents. She was enjoying her adventure with her group of friends, but most especially, she enjoyed her boyfriend's antic attention. She didn't want it to end. She could ride forever with Rick, away from her domineering parents.

Lizza road past them making a rude remark, "Get a room. Cool it down you two. You look ridiculous, like teenagers in puppy love."

Suzanne looked doleful, and that set Rick into retaliation on Suzanne's behalf.

"HEY, KNOCK THAT OFF, LIZZA," Rick shouted at her. "YOU'RE JUST JEALOUS BECAUSE YOUR EX WAS SUCH A LOUSE. DON'T TAKE IT OUT ON US."

"I'm sorry Suzanne," Lizza mumbled back quickly. She was red with embarrassment. She tapped her horse gently with her heels to get her steed to move quickly past the two lovebirds.

It was true; Lizza was jealous. She was hopelessly in love with her ex. She couldn't even say his name. No one in the group of friends dared to mention Lizza's ex boyfriend's name. They all realized by watching Lizza's numbing stupor that she was more than infatuated with her ex. They didn't understand the extent of her pain in the humiliation of her ex and their sorority sister, not until she started acting daffy. Her friends believed that it was taking Lizza way too long to get over the humiliation of her ex's deceitful infidelity.

Lizza's thoughts wandered as she rode numbly along with the others. *I was faithful to him. I'm pretty, and I'm popular. Why would he do this to me?* On and on, those thoughts kept repeating in a mazed stupor as she rode blindly behind the entourage. Each time the consortium stopped for a rest, Lizza sat alone away from the group. She would not talk with anyone. Alex tried many times to make conversation with her, but Lizza was always in a daze, not in reality.

"Alex, keep an eye on your friend, Lizza. I'm worried about her. She doesn't look well." Dick suggested to his daughter.

"Yeah, Dad. You're right. I think something is wrong with her. I just can't put my finger on it. I'll keep an eye on her. Thanks, Dad." I said as I kept a constant vigil on all my companions.

I felt it my duty to watch over my friends. This was a new adventure for all of us and I knew that I was the only one, beside my father, who was experienced enough to pursue this perilous expedition, except for Brian, he seemed to adapt at almost all his endeavors. I was pleased that my friend Brenda had found a decent man that loved her as I felt that my friend deserved.

What did I get my friends into? I thought while riding past each member of my consortium as I checked in with each one individually. I rode back and forth several times during the day checking on my sorority sisters and their boyfriends. I felt deeply responsible for their welfare, and this was just the first day.

When the team first started out, they were busy chatting with each other about any subject that would pop into their heads. Now, eight hours later and roughly twenty miles of easy terrain riding into the wilderness, they were all ready for bed. They were almost too tired to groom their horses. Since this was their first night, a pattern had not yet been established for their camp set up. Dick, Alex and Brian offered to help everyone else with their horses and with their prearranged chores to help complete their tasks that were assigned to them. They were so tired that they didn't even want to cook supper for the first night. All they wanted was to rest their bodies that ached in places they didn't even know that they could ache.

Dick called the spot for their first night's interval. Dick, Alex and Brian set up the mini tents in a circle. Rick and Brian shared one tent, and Suzanne and Brenda were in another. Dick refused to let the couples sleep together throughout the expedition, especially for Effram and his daughter. Effram and Dick shared a tent together, and Lizza and Alex shared the last tent in the circle. They looked like an old wagon-train campsite with the horses and mules tied to a tether line as the pioneers corralled in a circle.

Brenda was actually in a good humor. She had recouped faster than the rest of the group since she was dismounted from her horse and not irritated by riding. She prepared supper for the entire group. Brian found out that Brenda was also a very good cook and could improvise with even the most bazaar kitchens, even at a campsite setting. He was really proud of his "dumpling," his endearing pet name for his lover. At first, Brian thought that Brenda would be offended with the endearing pet name, but Brenda, who was very confident in her character and femininity, loved her endearing pet name that he had for her. It was a special endearment between the two of them that no one else could or would understand.

Brenda found some corn meal and several cans of pinto beans and prepared a delicious meal for everyone before we all retired for bed.

Effram and I groomed the mules together, since the horses were done earlier with Brian's and Dad's assistance. Brian and Dad left Effram and me to finish up the grooming of the mules so that we could have some alone time. I guess they both realized that I needed some time alone with Effram. Effram was exhausted, but he always had time and strength to kiss me.

"Effram, will you be all right with my dad in his tent?"

Effram nodded in consent. He didn't have a choice. Mr. Bush dictated the assigned sleeping arrangements before he had a chance to rebuttal. In some small way, he felt relieved not to have the pressure of abstaining from his sexual desires while in her father's presence. It wasn't just the pressure of being a gentleman before Mr. Bush, but it was also the pressure of being truthful to his chosen field of his life's work—his choice to be a minister in the face of his Lord and Savior. He had struggled so long already to deny himself the pleasures of the woman he chose to be with in his life. He hadn't asked Alex to be his wife. He felt that it was too soon for him to put her in that situation. He tried to think of the outcome of any quandary in her perspective first before he allowed his desires to emerge. On this adventure, Mr.

Bush had helped him, and he was grateful of the lack of pressure for an embarrassing situation.

"I'll be fine, Alex. What about you? You have to bunk with Lizza. I've been watching her today, and she doesn't seem to be acting normal. She's been awfully quiet and subdued all day. Be careful with her. She could go off the deep end. I don't think she's gotten over …" Alex stretched her right arm toward Effram's face and put a finger over his mouth. Effram stopped his thoughts before he could mention Lizza's ex-boyfriend's name.

"Please don't mention his name. We're all so very upset with Lizza's ex, and we promised her we would never say his name again. It's our way of supporting her." Alex tendered faithfully.

"Okay, I won't, but you need to be careful. Sometimes people do odd things when they're distraught."

"I will." Alex moved in closer toward Effram and began to kiss him amorously. She didn't want to talk about Lizza anymore. She wanted to be more passionate with her kisses, but she knew he would not compromise her while her father was nearby. So, she settled for his gentle amorous kisses before they returned to the campsite.

While Alex's consortium was sleeping peacefully in their bivouac, a lone stranger was spying on them from a distance. He used a modern world-class crystal-clear binocular to keep close observation on the entire team. The binoculars were equipped with day-and-night vision which also had an obsidian core with high-resolution accessories.

The stranger deliberately set up his camp several miles away from the Bush family's expedition team. He had been surveying the Bush family since he read about the death of Len Hudson in the local newspaper several weeks earlier.

No one knew about the stranger who followed the Bush consortium. He kept himself secretly and totally at bay, temporarily, from Len Hudson's fortuitous family. At this time, no one knew of the stranger's incensed desire to physically harm each and every one of Len Hudson's expedition team, especially Len Hudson's immediate family.

Chapter

SEVEN

Alex awoke early before the entire entourage. She felt it her duty to be the team leader for her adventurers, since the only reason they were on this wild western revelry was to help her complete her grandfather's final bequeath on his dying bed: to retrieve her grandfather's buried gold.

"LET'S GET GOING. COME ON EVERYONE. DAD SAID WE MUST PUT IN AT LEAST TWENTY-FIVE MORE MILES TODAY. AND WITH AS MANY STOPS AS WE'VE BEEN TAKING, WE NEED TO GET STARTED. WE DON'T' WANT TO SET UP CAMP IN THE DARK. WE COULD END UP IN A RATTLESNAKE PIT. WE SURE DON'T WANT THAT TO HAPPEN." Alex announced loud enough for all to hear.

Just the word *rattlesnake* made Lizza flinch. Snakes were her number one phobia, not that she had many, but she had feared snakes ever since she was eleven years old. Lizza stared at the roof of her tent remembering a trauma event where her younger brother Ralph, who was age eight at the time, had died by several snake bites. He was playing in the garden at their grandmother's suburban countryside home. She remembered standing at the edge of her grandmother's garden yelling at her brother and ordering him to "get out of that vermin pit before you get bit." Just as she hollered, Ralph picked up a snake that had slithered over his shoes.

Lizza remembered her brother saying, "Look Lizza, here's one of those vermin now." She remembered, so vividly, Ralph holding the rattlesnake by its tail instead of by its head. She saw that Ralph had no control over the snake. The snake hissed a few times while Lizza shouted for Ralph to throw the snake, quickly, but Ralph was not quick enough. The rattlesnake had bitten Ralph several times, and each time it bit Ralph, it planted potent venom. Lizza watched her brother die from the rattlesnake bites. She watched her brother's arm swell severely as his body shook in convulsive jerks. He immediately began to vomit and then he bent over with agonizing abdominal pain. She hollered for her grandmother and her mother, but they did not hear her calls. By the time she ran in her grandmother's house to get to her mother, Ralph was in a coma. It had taken Ralph several days to die. Lizza refused to leave his side, even in the hospital. She lay beside Ralph in his hospital bed until his dying end. Oh yes, rattlesnakes were Lizza's worst fear.

Lizza smelt the fresh coffee brewing that had everyone else in the expedition moving. They all became motivated and synchronized with the smell of the coffee percolating on a campfire that was erected on a temporary pit. Bedrolls were tied properly to their saddles. The tents were swept clean, folded, and packed onto the mules. A simple breakfast was made, eaten, and utensils also packed away on the mules.

"Good job, everyone." Dick announced. He wanted to be gone from their first camping spot as soon as the sun rose. It was cooler to ride in the early morning breeze. By midday the sun was scorching hot.

Most of their travels would be in the early morning, just after a good night's rest. However, no one slept a good night. Alex heard everyone complaining about their lack of sleep. Only three of them got a good night's rest: Dick, Alex, and Brian. Brian was used to horseback riding, since he once had a part time job as a horse groomer and stall cleaner for an entire summer. He's had so many peculiar, odd jobs that none of his jobs bothered him anymore. He always slept like a newborn baby.

Brenda began whining as soon as her rump hit her saddle. Brian winked at her, but she just ignored him and kept on whining.

Lizza had been watching meticulously for snakes ever since she heard Alex's comment. Now besides being in a stupor with lachrymose eyes over her self-pity of having a cheating boyfriend, she now had become paranoid over her fear of snakes. Her days and her nights were miserable. There was nothing Alex could say or do to help her relieve her misery.

Alex knew that she had to keep motivating her adventure consorts forward until she retrieved the buried treasure, the twenty bags of gold. She had to leave Lizza to her misery. Alex periodically checked on Lizza, but she never interrupted her personal anxieties. Effram had promised Alex that he would also try to keep an eye on her as well. Effram had mentioned to Alex that he thought that Lizza was acting even stranger today than she was yesterday. Alex agreed and they both watched her candidly.

The couple that was truly enjoying the excursion the most was Rick and Suzanne. Rick was Suzanne's strong, athletic horseman. Her handsome wrangler who doted on her every move. He rolled Suzanne's bedding. He folded Suzanne's and Brenda's tent. While Rick was doing all this for Suzanne, she gathered coffee and mustered lots of food for him. They were acting like honeymooners, except that they had separate sleeping arrangements. They were planning to fix that arrangement with Brenda and Brian and swap their sleeping partners for the duration of the expedition. This was Suzanne's first time, ever, to freely enjoy herself without constant pressure from her parents. Suzanne was like a naughty little girl that could steal cookies from a cookie jar without the fear of getting caught. She couldn't believe that her parents allowed her this vacation away from school. Suzanne was twenty-one, and knew all her legal and moral ramifications, but her parents had such a strong mental control over her that she would never disobey their commands. Suzanne took every opportunity to enjoy herself during her first and probably her last vacation as long as her parents lived.

Alex let Suzanne have her fun, naughty as it may become, but she never interfered with Rick and Suzanne. Alex would not allow anyone else to tell them otherwise. She knew of Suzanne's parents, she had met them on several occasions, and she also was amazed that her parents let Suzanne come with her on her quest. She thought that maybe her parents saw how burnt out she was with life, and thought that she might do something stupid, like end it all. Whatever reason her parents had to let Suzanne take a vacation, it worked for Suzanne. She was having the greatest time of her life with her boyfriend, Rick.

Later that afternoon, Alex rode side by side with Effram as often as she could. They talked about his future. Effram talked about his dreams and high expectations in life. He wanted to be a minister for low-income families with teenagers. He wanted to direct the youth of the world toward God. Alex admired that in him; however, she wasn't crazy about moving to a foreign nation, if they were to marry. She convinced him that he needed to help teenagers right here in America. She was willing to travel all over the United States with him. She figured that it would only take a few hours on an airplane ride from anywhere in the United States to return home to her parents, her horses, and her beloved mountain ranges.

The group was traveling smoothly on the directed path toward their destination with Dick Bush in the lead. Most were riding in pairs, except for Lizza. She started to slow down and let herself lag behind everyone else. She was alone and the last person on the trail.

Everyone was so caught up in their own conversations and in the monotonous ride that no one saw a stranger ride up behind Lizza. Absolutely no one saw the stranger place a very large rattlesnake onto Lizza's saddle. After the deviant intruder dropped the snake, he pulled on his reins and rode off in another direction. The stranger dismounted and tied his horse to a bush, then he planted himself with his binoculars. He fixed his gaze on the young woman who was lagging behind the others. He wore a large grin. Then he waited to watch the bedlam that was about to occur, which was almost too apprehensive for him. He scanned the area through his binoculars and watched the rattlesnake slithered over the saddle bags, up and over the back side of the girl who was acting stranger than the others. His grin froze upon his face as he heard the scream. The strange girl's scream. His heart was beating quickly, and his thoughts were disdainfully pleased. Lizza screamed so loud that the rattlesnake froze before it fell from her shoulder. The horse could smell the scent of the snake, and with fear for its own safety, the horse began to rock and buck. Lizza, who was still a greenhorn on a horse, could not hang on to a bucking horse.

She was thrown into the air before she landed right next to the very large and very aggravated rattlesnake.

Dick rushed to Lizza's aide the moment he heard her scream. The rattlesnake coiled in a striking pose, its rattles were shaking imminently, and it was ready to thrust its fangs into Lizza's leg. Dick appeared with his pistol in hand. He aimed and shot twice. The first shot hit and killed the snake, and the second shot pushed the snake away from Lizza's vicinity. Lizza screamed again. She shook with extreme fright. Dick climbed down from his steed and grabbed Lizza and held her until her body stopped shaking.

"There was a…a…a s-s-snake on my s-s-saddle," Lizza stuttered with pain and fear. "It slsl-slithered onto my b-b-back. I felt it creeping up tor-tor-toward my head. I s-s-screamed, and the s-s-snake fell to the ground, then my horse b-b-bucked me off." Lizza explained her perilous plight precariously. She was in shock, but she added another hint as to what she saw as she started to control her stuttering, "I think—I saw—someone riding—past me—before I fell," she stated in short breaths. She was so engulfed in the incident that she didn't even realize the pain from her broken leg. She broke her left tibia bone when she fell from her horse.

When I rode up, Dad stood up and left Lizza in her dazed bearing and walked toward me. "Alex," Dick addressed his daughter. He whispered to her so only she could hear him. "Lizza broke her leg. We've got to clean it and reset it now before it starts to heal in its broken state."

"What! What happened, Dad?"

"I'm not sure. Lizza said she thought that she saw someone ride past her, then a rattlesnake frightened her horse and bucked her off. She broke her leg when she fell. Do you think it was one of your friends that rode past her?"

"No, Dad. I'm positive. Everyone was riding with a partner, except for Lizza who was lagging behind. I was with Effram, Brenda and

Brian were side by side in front of us, and Suzanne and Rick were riding while holding hands."

"Well, then"—Dick stopped talking for a brief moment and turned to watch Lizza for a few seconds before he turned to address Alex again— "we've got to figure out how this happened, but we've got to reset her leg first. Go see if anyone of your friends will help us with this."

"Sure, Dad." I turned and shouted for everyone to dismount and gather nearby.

Effram rode up first, "What happened, Alex?"

"Just a minute. Let's wait for everyone to gather before we discuss Lizza."

Effram and I stood by our horses holding their reins. Everyone else dismounted and followed my lead.

"Lizza fell from her horse and broke her leg. I need someone to help Dad reset her leg."

Brian volunteered first, "I've got some experience in doing that. I took a course in some EMT classes. I had to reset a student's arm when he fell from the McGregor's stables."

"Thanks Brian. Anyone else?"

"I can help," Rick yelped. "I've broken my leg and my arm before in football games. I'm a fast healer."

"I'm glad to hear that," Alex said. "I mean, I'm glad that you've got some experience in this matter. I didn't mean that I was glad that you got hurt. You know what I mean, don't you, Rick?"

Rick laughed, "Yeah, I do Alex. Don't sweat it. Let's get Lizza fixed up."

Everyone gathered around to help or to watch. Lizza's adrenaline was soaring, which Dick thought was a good thing to help her with the next step that was going to happen.

Suzanne ran to the mules and fetched the emergency kit that was packed away.

"Thanks, Suzanne. We'll need those bandages." I retorted.

Lizza screamed again, when the improvised emergency volunteers reset her leg, and then she passed out. Alex caught her head just before it hit the ground. From a distance the stranger was laughing while he observed the entire chaos from his binoculars.

Dick thought he heard a sound echo from the woodland. *Laughter, did I hear laughter?* Dick didn't share his thoughts with anyone else, not at that time. He just wanted to dress Lizza's injury.

"What are we going to do, Dad?" I asked.

"We'll have to set up camp here. I wanted to be a few more miles closer to the overcliff that is marked on your grandfather's map. However, with this setback with Lizza's injury, I think we should settle here for the night. At least, until we see how Lizza is doing in the morning."

"Do you think Lizza will be able to ride?"

"I don't know. First, we have to wait until she wakes up. If she doesn't wake up on her own, well then, it's obvious that we will have to tie her to her horse in a way that she can't fall off and take her to a hospital as quickly as we can. If she wakes up on her own, well, we'll just have to wait and see what we will do next," Dick reported to his daughter.

"I'll inform everyone, Dad, that we have to settle here for the night and possibly longer if we need to. We'll get the tents and everything else set up while you finish up with Lizza." I turned quickly to gather my consortium and brief them on our impending status. Effram grabbed me and hugged me. Brain and Brenda also hugged each other. Rick grabbed Suzanne and hugged her as well. They were all so very concerned about Lizza's health and with one another's mental distress. Actually, all the men were grateful that it wasn't their girlfriend who fell off her horse and broke her leg.

Dick approached the group and said, "Lizza will probably sleep the rest of the day. We have to wait to see how she's doing before we can move her."

Everyone nodded in agreement with Mr. Bush's assessment of the situation.

Mr. Bush started popping orders. "There's a cot on the last mule on the tether line. Brian, will you go get it and set it up for Lizza? Then you and Rick carry Lizza to her tent and gently put her on the cot. The girls will take over from there and make Lizza more comfortable."

No one said a word for the rest of the day while they all chipped in to make their campsite suitable for the evening, not until they finally settled in for the night. It wasn't until everyone was in a circle for dinner before the conversation burst into questions.

"What happened, Mr. Bush?" Effram asked. He felt more comfortable calling him Mr. Bush rather than Dick as did the rest of the group.

"Truthfully, I'm not sure." Dick answered.

I was walking toward the campsite and sat on my saddle as a stool that was placed around the campfire. "I just checked on Lizza. She's still unconscious. She's been out since we reset her leg early this afternoon. Isn't that scary, Dad? I thought it was wrong to be unconscious for so long after an injury. It could put her in a coma." I suggested.

"Yes, usually that's correct. I don't think that it's all that wrong in her case. I think that the more she's out, the better it will be for her to recover." Dick offered his advice.

Dick looked at Alex and mentioned something even more upsetting. "If she doesn't wake up soon, we will all have to turn around and return home."

Suzanne jumped in with her comments. She didn't want to end her vacation just yet. She was enjoying her freedom away from her domineering parents, and she was loving her doting boyfriend. "If she wakes up, do you think we could continue Alex's quest?"

"Probably." Dick premised. He also wanted to fulfill his daughter's mission, but not at the risk of her friend's life.

"Let's take a vote." Rick proposed to support Suzanne.

"There will be no vote until we see if Lizza wakes up from her unconscious state." Dick bellowed.

"Yes, sir." Rick said apologetically. "I didn't mean anything sinister, Mr. Bush."

"I know Rick. We all want Alex to complete her mission, but we have to be concerned about Lizza's health."

"How much further do you think we need to go?" asked Brian.

Dick picked up the map and studied it for a few minutes, and then stated, "I would estimate that we could be there in two more days. Maybe a day and a half, according to this map. I can see the tree line that is mentioned on this map with my binoculars. So, I guess, it's probably about another day and a half's ride from here."

I spoke up next, "I'll keep an eye on Lizza tonight. If she wakes up tomorrow, and she agrees that we can move on, then we will, but if she doesn't wake up, well then, we definitely must go back and get her to a hospital. Is that agreeable to everyone here? If Lizza doesn't wake up tomorrow, then we must cancel this expedition and return home."

It was a unanimous vote. They all agreed with Alex's decision. It was her quest in the first place. They all agreed that she should set the motion of the agenda.

"Mr. Bush, may I speak with you a moment, please?" Rick asked, a bit bashful.

"Yes, Rick. What can I do for you?" Mr. Bush answered.

The tall muscular football player was pushing dirt with his boots and stuttering as he tried to tell Mr. Bush that he was going to switch tents with Suzanne and Brenda for the evening and for the rest of the trip. He informed Brian that he wanted him and Brenda to occupy a tent while he and Suzanne shared the other tent. Brian had no qualms with that arrangement. Now Rick was informing Mr. Bush of the switch. Rick didn't want to make the switch behind Mr. Bush's back. He respected Alex's father and believed him to be an honorable man. He just wanted to be with Suzanne, day and night.

"Thank you, Rick, for doing the manly thing and letting me know what you are about to do. You are twenty-one and I can't stop you. I feel it is my duty to warn you about safe sex, and unwanted pregnancies," Dick offered in return.

"We realize that sir. Suzanne and I have been going together for over a year now. We're very careful."

Dick asked Rick one more question to ease his thoughts before retiring for the evening.

"Is Brenda and Brian in agreement with your switch of tents?"

"Oh, yes sir. Brenda and Brian have also been going together for a very long time too.

They are also very careful." Rick answered with a grin on his face.

"I see," said Dick. "Well, thank you again for informing me of your actions."

Dick turned and joined Effram in his tent for the evening. Alex retired in the same tent where Lizza was still unconscious but resting peacefully.

While everyone else was settled in their tents, and before Dick settled for the night, he quietly stepped out of his tent, and with his pistol in his holster strapped to his side, he patrolled the perimeter of their campsite. His thoughts were heavy on the disturbing noise that he thought he had heard from a distance when they had reset Lizza's left leg. Dick thought to himself, *I know that I heard laughter in the bushes. Who would do such an evil thing?*

Dick continued to check on the horses and mules and made sure the tethers were secured. Then he completed his safeguard sentry around the campsite. As he ambled past the peripheral area of their settlement, he placed some twigs in a crisscross pattern interspersed throughout the campsite so to alert him if they had an unwanted visitor in the night. When he finished his patrol, he quietly slipped back into his sleeping gear and fell sound asleep. Before he dozed off, he placed his holster and pistol at his arm's reach.

Chapter
EIGHT

Everyone awoke anxious to see how Lizza was holding up. I got up early and started a fire to get the breakfast ready, especially the coffee. It seemed that the smell of fresh-brewed coffee was the motivating element that got everyone up and about.

"Good morning, Alex." Effram whispered in Alex' ear as he grabbed her from behind and wrapped his arms around her waist giving her a gentle hug, then he kissed her on her neck. Alex turned around and wrapped her arms around his neck and kissed him affectionately on his lips. The response was genuinely romantic, and they both felt love bursting throughout their being.

"Good morning Effram. Did you sleep well with Daddy?"

Effram grunted but placed a grin on his face. "Your dad's okay. I was so tired last night that I believe I was totally out cold before your father returned from his rounds on checking on the animals. I didn't even hear him come into the tent."

Dick Bush stumbled out of his tent a little while after Effram, giving Alex and Effram a moment alone. Before he greeted his daughter, he grunted and wheezed, clearing his throat. He was trying not to interfere with his daughter's time with Effram. He stumbled over a small stack of fire kindle as he tried to ignore the romance that was being exchanged between his daughter and his tentmate. Effram and Alexandria both acknowledged Dick's obvious nasal antics during his approach. They both laughed at Dick's clumsiness in his attempt in trying not to seem to be bothered by their romantic affection.

"Good morning, dear. How does Lizza look this morning?" Dick asked in a caring and gentle voice, and then he greeted Effram, with a bit more directness in his greeting. "Good morning, Effram."

Effram and I nodded our heads toward Dad, and then I said, "Good morning, Dad. She's still not awake yet. I thought that I would try to wake her up when breakfast is ready. I'm sure she'll be starving if she comes around." I suggested.

Just then Brenda and Suzanne came around to the campfire. Brenda's hands were full of tortillas, and some canned goods that she was going to prepare for breakfast. She even had some fruit in her hands that she planned to slice up for all to eat.

"I heard what you said to your dad," Brenda said. "I'll have breakfast ready in about thirty minutes. You go see if Lizza can be aroused."

I returned toward Lizza's tent where I knew she was still sound asleep. I carefully knelt by Lizza's side and started to tap her shoulder, shaking her to awaken.

"Lizza, wake up. It's me, Alex. You've got to wake up now."

Lizza didn't budge, she didn't stir, and she didn't even twitch.

"Lizza, come on girl. It's time for you to wake up." I continued to shake Lizza by her shoulder.

I started to cry. I was terribly afraid that my girlfriend was in a coma. "Please Lizza, wake up now." Tears were running down my cheek and I didn't bother to wipe them away.

I tried to use a sterner voice. "Lizza. You open your eyes, right now. Do you hear me. Lizza. Open your eyes."

I held my breath and listened to Lizza's breathing. I couldn't hear any changes and there wasn't any movement on her cot.

"Lizza, please, open your eyes." I said while I was crying over her cot. I pleaded in the gentlest voice.

"Why are you crying?" Lizza asked.

"Oh, Lizza, boy am I glad to hear your voice."

"Well, why are you crying?" Lizza asked again.

"You've been out cold for a day now. Don't you remember. You fell off your horse and broke your leg."

"Oh, that's why I'm in pain. I can't remember a thing." Lizza stated more confused than in pain.

I asked, "You can't remember falling?"

"Nope."

"Well, how do you feel?"

"Except for the pain in my leg, I feel great. Have you got some aspirin I can take. I sure could use some. And boy am I hungry." Lizza bellowed with enthusiasm in her voice.

Alex stuck her head out of the tent and hollered for her father, "DAD. COME HERE. LIZZA'S AWAKE."

Dick rushed to Alex's tent and strutted inside. "Hi, Lizza. How do you feel?"

"Great, Mr. Bush, but boy am I hungry. Do you think I could get something to eat, and I sure could use some aspirins."

"We'll get you food and an aspirin immediately." Dick said with a grin. He was so pleased to see her awake and looking so good. You couldn't even tell that she had a broken leg, and that she was set up with a makeshift tourniquet.

Lizza tried to get up but tumbled back down onto her portable cot. "Hey, how'd I get this broken leg?" she asked.

"You don't remember anything?" Dick asked her.

"Nope."

Dick informed her of her fall. "You fell off your horse."

"Really. How'd that happen?"

"You sure you can't remember anything?" Dick asked her again.

"Nope."

"Just lay quietly on your cot, and we'll go get you some food and a couple of aspirins."

Dick motioned to Alex to follow him out of the tent and gathered everyone around to talk about Lizza's injury.

"What really did happen?" I asked, even though Dick explained the incident the night before. It appeared that I was totally confused about the accident.

"Dad, should we tell Lizza everything? You know, about the snake that caused her horse to buck her off, and that she broke her leg on her fall." I asked before giving Dad a chance to answer my first question.

"I don't think we should do that. You saw how she was acting in the past few days. Today, she seems fine. Even her broken leg is only giving her some minor pain. Hopefully the aspirin will help with that. Let's bring her out here and have her sit with us around the campfire for breakfast.

Suzanne asked, "We can always ask her if she wants to keep going to help Alex complete her quest."

They all agreed to let Lizza make the decision to move forward or to return to home base.

Everyone had waited for Lizza to wake up before they could find out more about her accident. But now Lizza had no memory of the incident. She was showing signs of temporary amnesia. They all agreed not to say anything to Lizza about any of her troubles, especially the incident with her ex-boyfriend. They all thought that it was best not to tell Lizza about any of the anguish that was in her past. They believed it would hinder her recovery. No one wanted to see Lizza miserable like she had been before her accident.

Rick and Brian went to Lizza's tent and said, "Knock, knock. Can we come in?"

"Sure. Come on in." Lizza said with a smile on her voice.

Brian offered their services. "Mr. Bush asked us to carry you to the campfire. Wrap your arms around my shoulder and around Rick's shoulder and hop on to the traveling human chair."

Lizza giggled as she did as she was told.

"Alex," Lizza beckoned, "I've got to go pee."

I smiled at her and told the boys to carry her out to a nearby bush, and then leave her there until she calls for them again, after she had finished with her personal hygiene.

The boys did as they were told.

Lizza giggled again. "ALEX," she hollered, "I'm sorry to ask for help, but I seem to be having some difficulty in pulling my pants down over the swaddle on my broken leg. Will you help me, please?"

I smiled at Lizza, and the rest of the group started to laugh at Lizza's jovial mood. I struggled with Lizza's pants as I tried to pull them over the tourniquet on her leg. I cut the material on Lizza's pants on the left leg. This made it much easier to remove her pants to accommodate her to do her bodily functions. When she was done, I quickly called the boys to return to carry Lizza to the campfire. Lizza giggled again.

The breakfast was ready, and it tasted great. Lizza ate a large portion of it and kept complimenting Brenda on her superb cooking. Brenda kept thanking her for the compliments.

"What should we do, Dad?" I asked my father because I wasn't sure what to do next. Do we move on, or do we return home?

Dick whispered to Brenda, "Brenda, you stay here and take care of Lizza. We need to talk about this with the others without Lizza present. I'll have Alex inform you later on what we've talked about. Is that okay with you?" Dick asked Brenda.

Brenda nodded and everyone walked away and gathered in a huddle near the horses and mules.

Dick took charge. "We can continue to the buried treasure, but I think something is amiss with our expedition."

"What do you mean?" I asked while everyone else was nodding with agreement to my question.

"Before Lizza passed out yesterday, she said that the rattlesnake was put on her saddle and that it had slithered up on her shoulder before she screamed. Then her horse bucked her off. I killed the rattlesnake, but how did it get on her saddle? She also said that she saw someone ride past her before she fell." Dick stopped and looked around in the distance scenery, then he turned back to the group and continued, "Just after we set Lizza's leg, I heard a sound in the bushes not far from where she fell. I didn't mention it yesterday, because there was too much commotion with Lizza's incident. I heard someone laughing. I think there is someone out there trying to hurt us." Dick disclosed his suspicions.

Rick and Suzanne both tried to convince Mr. Bush that he must have been hearing things, since no one else heard anything or seen anything unusual.

"Maybe you're right," Mr. Bush said, "But I think that if we do plan on moving forward, then everyone must pay close attention to their surroundings. Also, everyone will have to help out with the health care of Lizza."

They were all in agreement again. Mr. Bush thought that this was the most pleasing bunch of kids that he had ever worked with.

In the distance, several miles away from Alex's consortium lingered the stranger. A stranger who was spying on them with his very expensive crystal-clear binoculars. He watched them all with hate building in his mind's eye. A hate for anyone related to Len Hudson. A hate so strong that made him want to kill, to kill anyone who meant anything to Len Hudson. However, he knew that he had to take his hatred down a notch. He had to wait to see where Hudson's family was going. Why were they on this expedition? An expedition in the direction where Len Hudson had found his wealth. The stranger decided to watch Len Hudson's family. He knows that he has plenty of time to kill the entire group, one by one. He had already hindered the group with one lame traveler. He can do it again, at any time. He just had to wait for the right moment.

Chapter

NINE

Lizza was in good humor. Her broken leg didn't seem to bother her during her travels. She let her leg dangle over her saddle while she was astride her horse. She couldn't put her left leg into the stirrup, so she had to ride without the brace of the stirrup on her foot.

Both Rick and Brian had to carry her and lift her onto her horse each time she mounted. They also had to do the same when she dismounted. They also had to carry her to a bush for her personal hygiene, retrieve her when she beckoned them, and they also had to carry her to her tent when she was ready to retire. Lizza felt embarrassed each time the men had to carry her like a queen, but she couldn't walk not even with the makeshift crutches that Brian had crafted for her comfort and balance. The mountainous terrain was too uneven for her to manipulate without falling on her face. She tried several times to get a handle on her makeshift crutches, but she just couldn't get her body to cooperate with the crutches. The men never complained about their onerous task of Lizza's beck and call.

The girls took turns waiting and grooming Lizza. They also took over all Lizza's duties that were assigned to her at the beginning of their trek. Everyone chipped in to help so that they could move forward on Alexandria's quest to find her grandfather's buried gold.

Suzanne was the most grateful of the bunch. She was truly enjoying her vacation away from her parents, and her honeymoon-like holiday with her boyfriend. The expedition was turning out especially more pleasant since Rick had moved into her tent.

The third day was much more difficult to ride. The terrain was rough, rocky, and dangerous. The rocky cliffs were rugged and slippery. Several times the horses and mules slipped and slid on the rock fragments, and on the loose rubble and bedrock that jetted loose from under the horse's hoofs.

Brian rode right next to Brenda to reassure her that she was becoming a true cowgirl.

She hadn't fallen off, not once, during the entire jaunt of the rugged terrain.

Brenda stopped whining and concentrated on her horse during their difficult trek. The sounds of the rocks sliding down the slippery slope didn't escape Brenda's keen hearing. Every time she heard a rockslide, she cringed with fear of falling down the steep slanted incline. She let go of her reins and let her horse do all the work. Brian congratulated her on being smart enough to figure out that the horse knows how to walk in difficult countryside. Brenda explained that it wasn't that she understood that the horse knew how to walk through the difficult turf. The reason she let go of the reins was because she wanted her hands to cover her eyes while the horse carried her through the slippery incline.

Once they passed the rugged ridge and riding became smoother and more enjoyable again, they all relaxed for over an hour before moving on again. Mr. Bush had announced during their break that they were almost at their destination. They would have to camp only one more night before they reached the overcliff that was marked on Alexandria's map.

"X marks the spot," Alexandria joked while everyone showed signs of excitement for being beyond their midway point on their expedition. They were all exhausted and ready to return home. It had only been three long, enduring days at this point of their trek, but they still had one more interminable day before they actually reached their final destination. Numbly, they all trudged along.

At sunset that evening, Dick drank some coffee while staring into the mountain wilderness, watching for any movement. He was constantly keeping a look out for any strangers in the distance. Every now and then, he'd see a deer nibbling by a tree. A twitch of a deer's ear would catch his attention. It was a pleasure to observe the deer rather than a baneful assailant who may be watching them. He especially tried to be more alert during their last trek to the buried treasure, watching for any signs of an adversary.

The stranger kept his distance, but he was getting restless. He wanted to create a little more havoc to Len Hudson's entourage. And havoc was what he bestowed upon the Hudson family.

On the last night of the entourage's camping outpost, before they reached their final destination, the stranger slowly and quietly sneaked into the Hudson's campsite in the darkest hour of the night and placed several sharp-filed rocks in all of the horses' blankets without any detection from the consortium. Even Dick missed the stranger's creeping assault to their tethered horses and mules.

When the morning arrived, everyone was in good spirits. This was the day they would all reach their final destination. No one paid attention to their horses' apparatus, except of course, Dick, Alex and Brian. The three adept equestrians shook out their manta as is the proper procedure before setting it upon a horse. The reasoning for this normal procedure was to cautiously remove any insects or vermin that might have crawled onto the manta while it lay on the ground over night before it was placed upon the horse under a saddle. This old country routine would have also removed any sharp, threatening debris or rocks that would have been placed in the manta by unsuspecting strangers. Dick, Alex and Brian were safe since the sharpened rocks that were placed in their horses' blankets were shaken free when they proceeded to follow the old country routine. Brian also dressed Brenda's horse, and of course, he shook her horse's manta before he tossed it up onto her steed; therefore, Brenda was also safe. Since Lizza needed someone to saddle her horse, which Alex had been accustomed to doing since Lizza's accident, Lizza was also safe.

However, Suzanne and Rick forgot to do the old country proper procedure of shaking their blanket that Dick had taught them before they left the Bushes' ranch. They were not safe.

Suzanne and Rick kept up their romantic banter and totally forgot to follow the proper procedure in saddling their horse.

Suzanne's horse jumped when she tossed her blanket onto its back. Immediately her horse felt the difference in the blanket that was placed upon its back. Her steed was acting like a spooked horse. Suzanne did not understand this behavior and began to yell and cuss at her horse. She grabbed the saddle and tightened the cinch.

"What's wrong with your horse?" Rick asked.

"Hell, if I know," Suzanne replied.

Rick also threw his blanket upon his horse without shaking it, and his horse started acting just like Suzanne's horse. Rick's horse acted skittish and nervous with the feel of the rock on its back.

Suzanne mounted her steed and started to trot ahead of Rick. Her steed started bucking wildly as though it were in a rodeo the moment Suzanne's weight was settled in her saddle.

Rick tightened the cinch on the saddle of his horse, and then quickly jumped up on his horse to try to catch up with Suzanne. Now both horses were bucking wildly.

Alex and Dick both raced over to Suzanne trying to catch the reins of her horse before she was thrown from her saddle. Rick leaped off his horse and yanked down on his reins to steady his horse, but Suzanne wasn't as lucky. Suzanne was screaming in a high-pitched screech. This just set her horse into a frightful panic. Suzanne's horse bucked and jumped into a grassy meadow. Suzanne grabbed onto her reins and reached for the horn of her saddle for her dear life.

Rick watched with fear growing rapidly. He couldn't do anything to help his girlfriend, his lover, his sweetheart. He felt helpless as he watched her scream with every bronco busting jolt.

Dick and Alex ran their horses along the opposite sides of Suzanne's horse as Dick reached over and grabbed for Suzanne's waist and pulled her off the unstable horse, Alex reached for the reins that was connected to the horse's bit. Immediately Suzanne's horse quieted down to a gradual trot after Suzanne's weight was removed from her saddle. When Dick dismounted his horse, he ran toward Suzanne's horse. Alex continued to tether Suzanne's horse, while Dick quickly loosened the girth of the saddle. Dick removed the saddle and blanket from the horse. He checked out the saddle first and all seemed well, but when he checked out the manta, he found a sharp-filed stone stuck into the fold of the horse's blanket. Dick shook his head as he rubbed the pointed edge of the rock.

"What's wrong with our horses?" Rick inquired. Since he was a city slicker and not familiar with the protocol of an equestrian, he was confused as to why his' and Suzanne's horse went berserk.

"RICK," Dick shouted at Suzanne's boyfriend since he was a distance away from him. "REMOVE THE SADDLE AND BLANKET FROM YOUR HORSE. CHECK THE BLANKET, AND SEE IF THERE IS A SHARP ROCK EMBEDDED IN YOUR MANTA?

Rick did as he was told while everyone else watched.

"Oh, shit, look at this," Rick said.

"What is it?" Suzanne asked, still shaking from her frightening ordeal.

"It's a rock, Mr. Bush, but it looks like it's been filed to a sharp point on both ends. This damn thing must have been stabbing my horse when I tightened the cinch on the saddle strap on its girth. That poor horse must have been in severe pain." Rick was shaking his head in bewilderment.

"How did that get in there? I asked.

"I haven't a clue," Rick stated. "I'm really sorry, Mr. Bush. I wouldn't hurt your horses for any money in the world."

"I know, Rick. Go check on Suzanne." Mr. Bush urged.

"Alex, we need to talk." Dick said with some urgency.

"What's up, Dad."

"These two rocks were in the blankets of Suzanne's and Rick's horses' mantas. Someone deliberately placed them there to hurt those horses." Dick said with an angry tone.

"Why would anyone want to hurt our horses?" I queried.

"I told you the other day, I think there is someone out there spying on us and trying to harm us." Dick implied. "And I think that person came to our campsite late last night and placed these rocks in our horses' blankets."

"How come our horses didn't do the same thing?"

"Well," Dick was rubbing his chin and thinking as he spoke and then asked his daughter a question, "did you shake your manta before you placed it upon your horse?"

"Of course, I did. I wouldn't put a saddle blanket on a horse unless it was shaken first," I rebutted.

"I know you would, dear. And so did Brian and me. That's why our horses weren't hurt. I'll bet that Suzanne and Rick both forgot to shake their mantas and the filed rocks were stuck into their horses' blankets." Dick responded.

Dick wanted to know if there were sharp rocks near their horses. "Alex, go check were we saddled our horses. See if there are any sharp-filed rocks lying around where we shook our blankets."

Everyone walked over to where the horses were tethered, and they all looked through the rocks on the ground. Very attentively, Brian and Brenda kicked the gravel and scree around with their boots.

"HERE'S ONE," shouted Brenda.

"I've found one too." Brian announced. "It's got a sharp point on both ends of this one."

"Do you believe me now?" asked Dick.

Suzanne and Rick started to nod their heads before anyone else.

"Why are we being persecuted?" I asked.

"I don't know, but I suggest that we all be very careful from now one until our trek is over. Pay attention to your surroundings. Keep a lookout while you are riding. If you see anything moving out in your horizon, holler for us to check it out." Dick was being overly cautious, but everyone was agreeing with him.

Suzanne wasn't sure she wanted to continue on with the quest anymore. "I'm ready to go home now," she said, a bit nervously with her voice in a quiver. Even her masquerade honeymoon sabbatical away from her overly controlling parents wasn't enough to deter her fear of the threats of physical harm.

Dick suggested, "Okay, Suzanne, we'll start home tomorrow, but today we go forward to complete Alex's quest. It's only a few more miles ahead of us. We can be there by late this afternoon. We'll dig up Len's buried gold, and then we'll leave first thing in the morning. How does that sound to everyone?"

Brian spoke up immediately, "It's fine with me." He didn't want to miss out on his bag of gold. He really needed that money for his college tuition.

Rick helped Suzanne saddle her horse. This time, he shook his and Suzanne's mantas before he placed them on their steeds.

Not far from Alex's consortium, hiding behind some ponderosa pine trees and a thicket of piñon and juniper trees and bushes, along a wall of woodland trees, and just past the grassy meadow where Suzanne's horse started to run and buck was the stranger spying on the Hudson family. He was holding his binoculars securely with both hands, watching the group. A smile grew across his face with total elation. He was completely satisfied with the havoc that he witnessed that he had caused with his own hands. He started to do a jig, and then he sang a weird song while he jumped up and down in jubilation.

The stranger watched the group pack up their gear and continue on their journey.

Where are they going? the stranger thought to himself. *What are they doing? I've got to know.*

Lizza was watching her surroundings intently, and she saw a flicker of light reflecting from the binocular lens in the distance along the forest tree line. She shouted, "MR. BUSH. MR. BUSH. OVER THERE BY THE TREE LINE. I JUST SAW A FLICKER OF LIGHT. MAYBE THE PERSON WHO IS TRYING TO HURT US IS OVER THERE?" Lizza was pointing in the direction of the flickering light.

The stranger saw the group gather together, and they were all staring in his direction. His heart started beating faster. He put away his binoculars and mounted his horse. Quickly he moved deeper into the forest of trees where the Hudson entourage couldn't see him anymore.

I've got to be more careful now. I think they know that I'm following them. That won't help them. Nope. Not one bit.

The stranger seemed very content with his morning viewing of the two horses' reaction to his mischief revelry from the night before. He was also very secure in his future plans to physically harm the Hudson group.

The stranger kept his distance but continued to follow the Hudson entourage.

Chapter

TEN

    The group saddled up and warily they left in single file following Mr. Bush's lead. Alex and Brian followed in the rear. Everyone was put on alert. It was a long, lonely ride for no one wanted to converse. The mood was gloomy for every rider, even Suzanne and Rick stopped their playful pretense honeymoon frolicking.

    As the day wore on in unspoken travel and nothing seemed out of the ordinary and no ominous threats were foreboding, the group continued as though they were in good spirits again. Brian caught up with Brenda and smoothed talked her into preparing a feast when they arrived at their final destination. Brenda was excited to think about food and what she was going to prepare for the group for their supper meal. Rick reached over and grabbed Suzanne's hand and they rode side by side for the rest of the trek, holding hands. Effram and Dick rode together in the lead.

    Dick was in constant watch for any intruders, and Effram was in faithful and devotional prayer. Alex rode with Lizza, while Lizza's memory gradually started to return. However, with the shock of the last two incidents that occurred with Lizza's broken leg, and the episode that happened earlier with Suzanne and Rick, Lizza didn't go into a hysterical fit, like she had in the past when she thought about her cheating ex-boyfriend. Instead, she talked with Alex throughout the duration of the trip and released some pretty heavy emotions onto Alex. Alex listened with minimal interruptions, and let Lizza spill her guts with empathy, embarrassment, and pain. The entire group was self-indulged that everyone reacted with surprise when Dick shouted with excitement.

"WE'RE HERE!"

The horses stopped. The overhanging cliff was in perfect view. Even the engraved rock where Len Hudson ascribed an epitaph for his deceased partner, Baxter Bartley, was in plain view. A quell solemness enraptured the group for several minutes before anyone dismounted. The mules and horses twitched and lurched restlessly until someone finally dismounted.

"Alex, let's set up camp before we try to find your grandfather's gold." Mr. Bush announced.

"Sure, Dad. Good idea. I don't want to set up in the dark," I agreed with my father. I hate setting up camp in the dark.

The horses were tethered, saddles were removed, and the gear dismantled from the mules. Alex and Brian attended to all the horses, while everyone else erected tents and sleeping gear. Brenda went directly toward the mules that carried the food supplies and was searching for the best meal ingredients. Lizza was put on cooking duties with Brenda now that her memory had returned. Everyone thought it best to keep Lizza busy so she wouldn't ponder so much on the SOB, Wayne, or her broken leg. Brenda enjoyed the company. She had a captive audience to her nonstop talking since Lizza couldn't get up and move away with her leg still in nature's improvised tourniquet. However, Lizza didn't mind listening to Brenda's constant chatter, she was grateful for having an avenue of solace from her own dreary thoughts. No one spoke to another person while chores were being executed except for Brenda, but Brenda thought that was part of her duties. She assumed that she was to keep Lizza comforted and amused.

Excitement to recover Len Hudson's buried treasure was building in everyone as they all continued their scheduled duties. No one wanted to be left out in the final retrieval of Alex's final quest: finding Len Hudson's buried gold.

After the delicious meal that was prepared by Brenda was over, excitement arose again to retrieve the buried treasure. The talk during the meal was only about Hudson's gold. Alex retold her grandfather's tales of his life's journey into the Mogollon Mountains, extracting of course her grandfather's confession of killing his partner. The group exchanged playfulness and pleasantries during the meal. Even the fear of a troublesome stranger didn't deter the excitement of the group in finding the buried treasure—the twenty bags of gold.

"Dad, I think we are ready to excavate Granddad's gold." I said.

"All right then," Dick said. "Let's get your map, Alex, and find where X marks the spot."

The girls giggled at Dick's cute quip. The men scattered to gather shovels that were carried by the mules. Dick glanced over the map and studied it carefully to find the exact place to start digging.

Mr. Bush counted 57 steps South of the engraved boulder. He pointed to a spot on the ground and stated, "Okay boys, start digging here." Brian, Effram, and Rick all started to dig in a large circle where Mr. Bush had indicated. At first the boys were digging rather hurriedly, but soon they wore themselves out. Effram stopped first and laughed at himself and at his friends.

"We must look like some old cowboy greenhorns in a frenzy." Effram said jokingly.

Brian nodded in agreement, "I sure feel like one." He laughed along with Effram, and Rick joined in with all the girls and Mr. Bush. They were all laughing in unison.

The atmosphere was jovial and relaxed, except for the sweat that was pouring down Effram's and Brian's faces. Rick didn't have any sweat running down his cheeks. I commented on this observation.

"Look at Rick! He's not perspiring at all. You gentlemen may want to leave the physical exertion for Rick. He seems more fit for this endeavor." I gestured.

Rick and Suzanne both were smiling with pride. Rick for his pride in his physical stature that he worked so laboriously to build, and Suzanne for her pride in her man. This was her boyfriend who is one of the all-star football athletes at the New Mexico State University and whom she knows loves her devotedly.

Mr. Bush interrupted, "I'm about to agree with Alex at this point. The hole is getting rather sloppy, and it may get more difficult to find the buried treasure with all three of you in it. I would suggest that only one of you should be digging at this point. I think you may be rather close to finding the gold."

Rick volunteered to continue since the other two were already sweating with exhaustion. It took less than five minutes before Rick struck something that deflected the shovel. Everyone was watching Rick intently when they all heard the resonant sound that emitted from the hole. They all held their breaths in silent anticipation. Every forceful movement that Rick exerted to uncover the awaited treasure, and every sound that echoed from the excavated aperture was pivoted with extreme intent in each one's emotions. Their desire of their share of the treasure that was offered to them by Alex, via her grandfather's legacy, was at that moment at a rapacious peak.

Rick shouted, "WATCH OUT," and tossed his shovel up and over the top of the hole's crevice. He carefully squatted and started to brush the dirt from the first lump that protruded from the bed of the hole. Slowly, Rick swept the dirt off each bag with his hands before he handed it to Alex and his friends who stood over the chamber.

"How many of these bags are down here?" Rick asked.

"There should be twenty bags in all." I replied.

"How many do you see?" Someone asked.

"Reach down and grab a bag as I lift them up to you." Rick ordered. He handed over a bag as quickly as he uncovered them from the pit that he was in. Effram suggested that they create an assembly line to extract the gold bags from the deep hole that engulfed Rick.

After a while, I informed Rick, "There should be four more bags still in that hole."

Rick kept digging with his hands and found all four of the remaining bags. Each bag was filled with gold nuggets, and each bag seemed heavy in weight. He tried to determine the weight of each bag before he lifted them up to be collected, but he was too excited to rely on his judgment. He did observe that each bag seemed to be in comparable weight. Already he felt a cringe of greed creep over him.

What the hell is wrong with me? Rick thought to himself as he stretched to lift the bags over his head to be collected by Alex's consortium. *I hate this feeling of greed. I don't want Suzanne to see me like this. I want Suzanne and me to live our lives together. I'll be picked for a circuit team, and Suzanne will be successful in her career. She's so good at everything she does, and she's so beautiful. I know that I'm not really smart, but I am good at football. I don't need this money. I just need Suzanne. She came along on this excursion to support her best friend, and I'm here because Suzanne wanted me to be with her. I will not let greed destroy what I have with Suzanne.* Rick pulled his thoughts together and jumped to reach the rim of the hole, and then he pulled himself out of the cavernous pit that hid the imminent hoard of gold for so many years. No one offered to help him out of the hole. They were all too busy fondling the twenty bags of gold.

Rick had changed in that pit. He was different when he pulled himself out of the dirt and gravel catacomb. He felt different. Greed would not crush his spirit. His love for Suzanne was much greater than the greed for a bag of gold. He also knew that this treasure was going to become a problem for all of them. He could feel it, like a sixth sense. There was evil attached to these twenty bags of gold, he could feel that too. He just didn't know how or why these twenty bags of gold were going to cause them endangerment, but he did know that he had to be very protective over Suzanne. Trouble was coming. Now he believed that his' and Suzanne's survival was much more important than Alex's quest.

In the distance, tucked away in the nearby timberline was the stranger spying on Len Hudson's family with his cherished possession of his world-class crystal-clear binoculars. He tightly gripped the binoculars with both his hands. His eyes were glued to the twist-up eye cups. The stranger grabbed the center focusing dual-locking optic knob to adjust his vision on his targets.

"What? What is this I see?" The stranger was now talking aloud to himself. "Oh my," he said even louder. "It looks like their digging for buried treasure. I see, yes, I see many bags coming out of that hole that they have dug. Now, what can be in those bags?"

The stranger started pacing back and forth, back and forth, past his horse. The sun was reflecting on the glass lenses of his cherished possession, generating a mirror of light. He was far enough away from the Hudson's entourage that he didn't care if they saw him now. More than anger was building in Buster's thoughts. He wanted more than revenge upon the Len Hudson family. He wanted possession of all their property, especially of their newly discovered treasure.

"I remember bags like that. I've seen those bags before. Oh, yes. I want those bags."

Evil thoughts were becoming clearer in his mind. Thoughts of destruction. Murderous thoughts. Thoughts of ambush and robbery, like in the old West when bandits robbed a stagecoach. Only he was just one man. All by himself.

"I must be one step ahead of them. I need to eliminate my enemy, one by one. I'll have to be careful. They're watching for me. I know they are. I've seen them stop and scan the terrain before they moved on in their travels. I've got to be ready for them as they return home. That's what I'll do." The stranger was talking aloud to himself, like a crazy, bewildered, madman.

The lone stranger noticed that the group had seen his reflection. He quickly lowered his binoculars and set them aside. *It doesn't matter now*, he thought, *I've got to be prepared. I want my revenge on Len Hudson's family, and I want their treasure. No. My treasure!* The stranger mounted his horse and slowly walked back into the forest timberline to hide his presence from Len Hudson's family entourage.

PART THREE

RETURN HOME: A REMORSEFUL TRIP BACK

Chapter
ELEVEN

The stranger packed up his gear and started to return home. He knew which trail Len Hudson's coterie would return. He had to prepare some ambushes to overcome them. His first crusade to accomplish his revenge was to gather some nature varmints, unusual critters, to help him punish the family of his nightmare nemesis. He wanted to hurt Len Hudson's family for the deviant deed that their patriarch had endured onto him and his mother, so many years ago. He felt that Hudson's family must share the blame for Mr. Hudson's actions. He believed that since Mr. Hudson was no longer living, then his family should assume Mr. Hudson's punishment. Nature did not allow Len Hudson to live any longer for retribution. The stranger cursed himself for not finding Len Hudson sooner. It was Hudson's obituary in the Chicago newspaper that finally led him to Len Hudson's family. How lucky he felt when he found the death announcement of a resident of Glenwood, New Mexico being picked up in the *Chicago Tribune* to report the death of one of their own.

This stranger has a name; it is Buster Bartley. He is the son that Baxter Bartley, abandoned along with his new bride to follow his dream of becoming a rich gold prospector.

Buster was but an infant when his father left with Len Hudson to become a gold miner. He had just turned eleven years old when Mr. Hudson had returned his father's remains. Mr. Hudson had given ten bags of gold to his mother along with his father's stiff, rotting dead body.

As if those ten bags of gold was going to ease his grieving mother's heart and soul.

Buster rode his horse slowly with agonizing regret, reminiscing on his childhood. He thought about the pain, the grief, and the hard struggle in his life that he had to endure without a father. Then just after he and his mother started working together with a routine of washing other people's dirty, smelly, bug-infested clothes and finding odd jobs to keep themselves in a home to survive until his father would return, they were given his father's dead, decomposing body. Buster remembered his mother watching the coroner unwrapping the corpse that had been returned by Mr. Len Hudson. His mother was asked to identify the body. He remembered gasping at the site of his father's remains. He saw rotted flesh flaking from his father's face, arms, and legs. The decaying smell was so rank that it made his mother vomit. This was how he saw his father for the first and last time of his life. He remembered seeing the fear, anguish, and disgust in his mother's eyes. Hatred engulfed him. His eleven-year-old mind was consumed with revenge toward Mr. Len Hudson.

Len Hudson, his father's gold-mining partner and the financier of his father's disappearance for years, came to visit his mother at their rented shack in the ghetto of South Side, Chicago. Their hut was located just off the main branch of the Chicago River, where most of the poor immigrants lived. The neighborhood was known as the "back of the yard" community. The crime level was extremely high. It was a neighborhood known for its disparity of income for the poorest of poor. They lived in a dwelling a little bigger than a native's tepee. It had only one room to accommodate both of them for their sleeping, bathing, and cooking. One bed was in one corner for Mrs. Bartley and a mat on the floor in another corner for Buster. There was a small kitchen table with one chair for his sickly, alcoholic mother and one wooden log used as a stool for himself. The stove was old and usually not fit for use. Buster had to chop wood daily to keep a fire going in the cracked potbelly on the many cold Chicago winter days and nights. Sometimes Buster would steal wood from the wealthy estates on the other side of town. When he was caught by the landowners for filtering slats of wood from the rich estate owners, they would beat him severely as his weak little body drew blood, scars, and pain, but they never offered compassionate help for him and or his mother.

Oh, but Mr. Hudson was so proud of himself for leaving ten bags of gold to help us get out of that bug-infested and dreary environment. But that's not what Mama did, Buster thought venomously. *No. Mama drank herself to death. I was an orphan by the time I was twelve. It took Mama only a year to drink herself to death and to let many men steal all those bags of gold. And those men took so much more from Mama. They took her dignity, they took her body, and they left her to shame. She couldn't look at me anymore. She hated me for being there. She saw me sitting on the porch each night when a man would come to our shack and abuse her. She hated me for being HIS son. The son of her husband who had left her and a newborn child alone for years to fend for themselves.*

Buster was fuming with hatred. His hatred was directed toward the surviving family of Len Hudson, the man who raised all the money to finance the partnership of two gold miners and then to leave him and his mother alone to fend for themselves for years.

Poor, poor Buster. He had to live in an orphanage until he was old enough to fend for himself. To steal, rob, and con as many people as he could to survive in this cruel, cruel world. There was no inheritance to come to him from his father's gold-mining days. All that gold was lost, stolen, and used to help murder his mother by booze and wanton men.

There was a short, chastened period in Buster's life when he met Molly Cartfeld. He was in his mid-twenties when he was admitted, unconscious, to the West Side Hospital in Chicago. During this period, the Presbyterian Hospital and the Rush Medical College merged together as an educational hospital. Chicago was in great need for medical providers. There were many nurses who belonged to a movement that wanted to reshape the healing process into a charitable mission with a religious order of nurses to help provide spiritual aid along with their nursing. Molly was one of those angelic nurses.

Molly nursed Buster to health. Their friendship bonded into something stronger and more romantic. Buster proposed matrimony, even though he was penniless, but Molly had a steady job. Molly convinced Buster that her wages could support them until he found a job. They got married and they moved in with Molly's parents. Molly got pregnant immediately, but the marriage did not survive. Molly divorced Buster and remarried. Buster lost all rights to his son, and Molly's new husband raised Buster's son as his own.

The campfire needed tending. Buster put a large log on the fire and stirred the embers, the burning tinder, with a long flitch. The fire quickly fluttered into a nice warm blaze. He gazed into the flames reminiscing some more on Molly and his son that he hadn't seen in years. It was all Len Hudson's fault. His life was doomed the moment Len Hudson met his father.

Buster pulled out a newspaper clipping from his pocket. It was the obituary for Len Hudson. He studied the names of the surviving family of Mr. Len Hudson. Slowly he read the names out loud, "Len Hudson is survived by his daughter, Mary Hudson Bush, married to Richard Bush, and their daughter, Alexandria, who all reside at the Bush equestrian ranch on the outskirts of Glenwood, New Mexico. The funeral will be held at the Ranchito Funeral Home in Silver City on Friday." Buster stopped there. He didn't read any further. He knew the date and time of Len Hudson's funeral. Oh, yes, he attended the funeral and behaved exemplarily, without malice. He wanted to see the faces of the family of his nightmare nemesis. He remembered, with a smirk upon his face, walking up to Len Hudson's family and offering his condolences for their loss at the funeral home. He thought inquisitively, how kind they were to him. They were so sad, yet they offered their gratitude for his presence at Len Hudson's funeral.

Now that he knew where they lived and he could identify Mr. Hudson's family from a distance through his precious binoculars, he spied on them endlessly. He hid in bushes, behind trees, and sometimes he lay on the ground for hours, spying from the thicket of ground-level sagebrush. He was persistent. He noticed some unusual activity stirring the entire household and the ranch hands. He didn't understand what was going on, but he could tell that they were planning on an excursion soon that included horses, mules, and quite a bit of traveling equipment.

Buster immediately left his spying sector and rented a horse and gear to travel into the wilderness for a month. He fabricated a story to the outfitter for the rental of a horse, mule, and all the equipment he needed for a month's journey in the wilderness. In his mind's eye, he thought it a kindred journey as his father's gold-mining jaunt. He offered a very large deposit to evade any questioning from the owner. It worked. He bluffed his explanations, and the outfitter believed his every word. Or the owner pretended to believe Buster's rubric to get the large rental deposit. Buster was familiar with greed overriding care and interest, for the rigger rented a very old mule and horse. The rigger would never miss the absence of these worn-out animals. Buster continued to stare into the lambent campfire. His thoughts of his hatred of Len Hudson extended throughout the night as he plotted and planned his next knavery mishaps that were to overcome the Hudson's family and their companions. Delight also encumbered his thoughts with the knowledge that he just may succeed in his revenge for his mother's namesake and for the misery that overshadowed his life. All because of Len Hudson's desire to become a gold miner.

Chapter

TWELVE

Morning came quickly for both camp sites.

Buster hurried with his chores. He repacked his saddle upon his horse, talking to the animal all while cinching the harness.

"I hate that family, and God knows that I want revenge upon each and every one of them. I hate them because their father destroyed my life. I hate them because Len Hudson killed my mother when I was only twelve years old. I hate Hudson for bringing my father's deceased, deteriorated body to my mother when I was eleven. You should have seen how my father looked in that most decrepit state."

Buster talked to the horse as though it were a human. He walked over to the campfire and doused it with his shovel, making sure it was completely out. "I don't want to cause a forest fire. Oh no. I sure don't have any animosity toward this beautiful wilderness. On the contrary, the wilderness has given me some peace. The wilderness has given me some enjoyment in my life. I could never get that from my mother. I was happy for a short while when I was married to Molly.

"If only I could have felt this peace and calmness with Molly, maybe I wouldn't have this bitter hatred for my deceased father's partner. I think my hatred is keeping me alive. Things will be much better for me once I get my hands on all those bags of gold that I saw them pull out of that hole." Buster was still talking to his horse. Every now and then, the horse would bob its head, which only helped Buster's fantasy that the horse was an impeccable listener.

Buster hurried with his outback tasks to gather the essentials for his third unmitigated, and revengeful attack on Len Hudson's surviving family. He totally understood his disposition, his hatred, and his craving desire for revenge. He truly believed that after Len Hudson's family accepted the punishment for the turn of bad luck that ravished his life, then his bad luck would be reversed, and happy times would finally enter into his life.

Quickly and bleakly, Buster contrived a devious plan to harm at least one more person in the group that he swore to torment, and hopefully kill. For his plan to work, to kill a member of the Hudson entourage, all the deaths had to look like an accident. Just like his father's death, when Len Hudson returned Baxter Bartley to his mother, who was pronounced dead by a wilderness accident. Len Hudson was never charged with his father's murder. Now he had to hurry to get to the mountain passage where the Hudson's mules and horses had trouble crossing a few days earlier. That was where he was planning his next deviant divergence. Buster rode hard for several hours before Alex's consortium began their trek. He was searching the desert for a den of scorpions. He was looking for sandy soil that was covered with noncompressed dirt and loose rocks. A general habitat for scorpions. He knew that the species of scorpions in the United States deserts were not really a serious threat to humans. However, he did know that if one was stung by several scorpions, maybe four or five scorpions, then the venom of all those scorpions could be a deathly threat to a human.

This was his plan. He would retrieve five desert scorpions and transport them to the slippery crossing by the rock junction that the Hudson's expedition would cross in just one day's ride. He had to hurry and find his bane: scorpions. He had to place them in a manmade hollow by the rock quarry where he observed the chunky girl slide down the rocky slope incline with her horse while her hands were covering her eyes and the horse's reins were loose. A frightened horse would buck, and a rider who has no control of her reins would definitely fall off, and possibly be stung by the many angry scorpions. *This is a good plan*, Buster thought in his crazy, mixed-up, malicious, psychosis with so much hate for his nemesis' family.

Buster enjoyed his plotting and planning of revenge. It helped relieve the pain of his memories. Memories that he blamed Len Hudson but never on his father, Baxter Bartley, who abandoned his mother and his newborn son to become a gold miner.

While Buster was off on his tantrum, Alexandria motivated her team to get ready for their return trip home.

The excitement rose giddily amongst Alex's consortiums. With the knowledge and expectations of returning home to safety and comfort, everyone was helping each other so to hurry the tasks at hand. The twenty bags of gold were distributed evenly between the horses and mules. All gear was packed on the mules, and each rider had their personal stuff packed, rolled and mounted onto their steed. The cleanup of the wilderness environment was immaculate, and done rather quickly, for everyone was very anxious to get started on their return trek home.

After everyone was ready and before they mounted to start their trek homeward bound, Alex read the epitaph that her grandfather had etched into the rock that designated the death site of Baxter Bartley aloud before their departure. She felt it was a befitting salute to her grandfather and for his partner who had died in the immediate vicinity some fifty years ago.

"Here's where Baxter Bartley departed this land. A gold miner, husband, father, and friend."

Alex remembered her grandfather's story where he had told her that he had to kill his partner to save his own life. She did not share this part of her grandfather's memories. She told them that this was where her grandfather's partner slipped and fell to his death by hitting his head on a rock. It was the truth; Baxter Bartley did die in that manner. She did ask Effram to give a spiritual blessing and a prayer for her grandfather, Len Hudson, and for his partner, Baxter Bartley.

Effram stepped up with pride for his chosen field of study as a minister and offered a memorable prayer of benediction to ease his girlfriend's trepidation. Alex smiled gratefully at Effram and politely thanked him for the beautiful prayer and salute for her deceased grandfather and his partner. She was delighted to hear Effram pray for a safe and uneventful trip home. She also had trepidation about their return trip home with a stranger at large. A stranger who was making horrible threats with harmful results to her entourage.

Before they all left, Brian drew a resemblance of the epitaph that was carved onto the large boulder under the overhanging cliff that honored the deceased friend and partner of Len Hudson. "Here's where Baxter Bartley departed this land. A gold miner, husband, father, and friend." Brian drew the scene so acutely that he even drew the resemblance of an embellished carving of a religious cross that Len had originally chiseled onto the boulder. No one had noticed the cross before this. Only the words stood out at the memorial. But Brian brushed the caked dirt away from the carving and drew a picture of the resting scene where Len Hudson had shown his respect to his friend and partner, Baxter Bartley. As Brian looked closer at the beautifully adorned carved cross, he noticed Baxter Bartley's name was engraved in the middle of the cross.

Effram was reading his Bible while he waited for the rest of the group to finish their chores. Alex had called for his assistance with Lizza's horse, so Effram placed his Bible upon the saddle of his steed. Everyone was so busy getting ready to leave that no one observed Brian placing the drawing that he just completed behind the back side of the hardbound cover of Effram's bible. Brian wasn't trying to be deceitful with his drawing, he just needed a safe, secure place to store his drawing until he could show everyone what he drew from their expedition. In all the commotion, with everyone getting ready to leave, Brian forgot about his drawing when he finished helping Brenda with her horse.

Before they all left to return home, Dick stopped to observe his surroundings. He watched carefully for any movements in the distance, in the dark of the forest, and in the brushes of the open fields. He didn't see anything unusual. He noticed a group of wild quail skitter under some brushes, and he thought he saw a doe peeking at them from the forest line. Then he realized that if he could see wildlife movements, then he knew that there were no humans in the vicinity. Animals have a keen sense of their surroundings, and Dick was relying on their acute perception.

They rode quietly for hours, following Len's map in reverse to find their way home. Even Brenda didn't whine or show signs of irritation while on her horse. No one even recognized Brenda's quiet mood, since everyone was in their own realm of thoughts. Everyone, even Buster Bartley was in his own realm of thoughts while he hastened to find five scorpions.

Chapter
THIRTEEN

Buster finally found the countryside where scorpions dwell. Carefully, while wearing thick leather gloves, he knelt on the ground near some soft dirt and loose slates and began to dig in the soft ground. Finally, several scorpions skirmished to the top of the dirt. Quickly, Buster jumped to the side and watched the scorpions run toward him. He grabbed seven scorpions by their tail, one at a time, that scattered in the vicinity where he was kneeling. He placed them all in a canvas bag and wrapped the tie enclosure closed securely. His horse quivered nervously with the scent of the scorpions. Buster was extremely pleased with himself, for his treacherous and conniving scheme that he had plotted was becoming tangible.

Before Buster left to the mountain ridge where the chunky girl slid, he walked toward his donkey and removed all the survival gear that he had brought with him from the small hacienda he rented near Glenwood. He had rented a little rancho-style casa near the Bush family when he read the obituary for Len Hudson to observe his nemesis family. He reached for his canteen, food, sleeping roll, and his trusty binoculars. He just let the rest of his gear plop to the ground, and it lay dormant where it fell, then he brushed the donkey's head and rubbed its ears before he slapped its rump. The donkey kicked a few times and rushed off into the wilderness. Buster pondered thoughtfully while he walked around the equipment on the ground, *my revenge is coming to a peak,* he thought to himself. *I do not need the donkey nor all this extra survival gear to finish my doomed destiny.*

Buster then stepped around all the survival equipment and mounted his steed.

He was not sure he would make it home alive either. He presumed that eventually, he would be caught and killed in his revenge attempts, especially with his bad luck that trailed him all his life. He had every intention on killing as many of Mr. Hudson's family before his demise, and if he could not kill them, then he wanted to maim as many as he could before his own death. His only distress was how he was going to get all those bags of gold that he planned to steal from the Hudson entourage to his son Brett.

He believed with all his might that he had no reason to live. His wife left him and remarried, and her new husband, Samuel Henson, offered to adopt his son. His ex-wife, Molly, needed his permission to allow her new husband to adopt their son, Brett Bartley. Buster gave his permission. He gave his only son away that very day that his ex-wife confronted him about the adoption. He felt that he was giving his son a new lease on life, a chance to break the curse of bad luck on the Bartley family. His son did not need to be burdened with the Bartley name, especially, when he fulfills his destiny of revenge for his father's and his mother's deaths. He knew that his name would be mud, if he were caught. *I've got to make sure that all their deaths look like an accident, just like my father's death was pronounced, death by a wilderness accident.*

Buster looked up at the sun and saw that his time was running out. He still had to make it to the rockslide where the Hudson team would be in less than three hours. He mounted his steed, secured the bag with the scorpions to the horn of his saddle, and then he rode hard and steady to the next jaunt where his hostile revenge needed to take place.

The sun was hot and beating down pungently. Buster was beginning to smell rancid from his sweat, but he had to hurry and keep riding hard. He still had to dig a small burrow by the rockslide, hoping to place the scorpions in the path of Hudson's entourage. He wasn't positive that the Hudson group would return home on the same path that they took to excavate Len Hudson's buried treasure. He had no other plan at that time, and he was quite pleased with his thoughts of using the scorpions as nature's weapon.

On his arrival of his destination, Buster scanned the rock incline carefully. He had to choose the right place to dump all the scorpions. It had to work. He didn't have another plan at the time. Slowly, he pushed some loose slates around with his boot until the soft dirt beneath the slate was unobstructed. He knelt down, and with both hands and a thick stick, he dug a hole and softened the dirt to almost a soft soil for planting seeds. He was satisfied with his work. He knew it was perfect soil for the scorpions to bury themselves. After he dumped all the scorpions from the canvas bag, he sat pondering on his meager thoughts from a distance by a thick mesquite bush, while waiting for the group to arrive. To occupy his time while waiting for Len Hudson's group to arrive, he watched the scorpions scurry about in preparing their new habitat in the rock incline with his trusty binoculars.

Buster's thoughts wandered. *I remember Mr. Hudson telling Mama that my father died of an accident in the mountains when he brought his body home for Mama to bury. Oh, how I would have loved to see Mr. Hudson die in an accident, but he's already dead. Someone has to pay for my father's death, and for my mother's death.* Buster was in full derange conversation with himself. His thoughts were always forlorn.

"I'm not a bad person. I've worked hard in my life. Mr. Hudson put this curse on my family and on me. I never had a father. Not one of Mama's boyfriends ever wanted to talk to me. They just wanted to use Mama. Poor Mama, she wanted my father to return so badly. If only he did." Buster spoke aloud for all of the trees in the forest to hear.

Buster stopped talking to himself and just stared into the Gila Wilderness, watching and waiting for the Len Hudson family to arrive. He was excited to watch another chaotic catastrophe strike the Hudson's family, and hopefully to kill or maim a direct relative of Mr. Hudson. In his spiteful state, he noticed the Hudson consortium approaching. He lay still on the ground covered by mesquite brushes. His camouflage was so good that he was completely invisible. Even the wildlife that nested in the area didn't notice him. Birds flew overhead, rabbits were hopping about, and insects were chirping until Hudson's group arrived. Buster watched in absolute silence. He knew that he could not make a sound, not even if his baneful plan worked. *It must look like a natural accident*, Buster thought apprehensively as he continued to spy on Len Hudson family.

Chapter

FOURTEEN

Dick Bush was in the lead as Alex's group rode in single file. They were approaching the rock incline where Brenda had trouble crossing in the beginning of their trek. Dick turned and hollered to the group.

"Okay everyone, ride with a partner. Maybe our horses will be more sure-footed across the rocks. If you see your partner slipping from their horse, I want you to stop your steed immediately. All of you follow suit, and all your horses will stop. If you all stop at the same time, the rider who is falling will be able to straighten themselves out upon their saddle. Does this make sense to all of you?" Dick watched the group nod their heads.

Dick was trying to make Alexandria's friends expert equestrians in one easy lesson. He was hoping and praying that they were paying attention and heeding his advice.

They paired up in their usual grouping. Brian with Brenda, Rick with Suzanne, Effram rode with me, and Dick rode with Lizza. Dick and Lizza rode along the rock incline first. They all waited this time until each one passed over the rocky incline. The slates were slippery, and the horses were nervous. The horses could feel the tension among their riders. Normally, a horse would trot over the terrain without any difficulty, but with the tension of their riders, and the accumulation of all the weight of their survival equipment and the added weight of the twenty bags of gold, the horses were struggling across the rocky grade.

Dick and Lizza crossed successfully and waited for the next paired set to cross the unstable slope. Rick and Suzanne went next. Rick wanted to hold Suzanne's hand, but Dick shouted, "DON'T DO

THAT." Suzanne jumped with Dick's shout and pulled her hand away from Rick. Rick straightened up on his horse and was going to protest rather angrily when Dick explained why before Rick had a chance to rebel.

"Rick, you'll cause Suzanne to slide to her right when she needs to be centered on her horse through this crossing. You too will be slanted on your horse when you should also be centered on your saddle."

"Sorry, Mr. B." Rick realized his mistake and felt bad that it could have been his fault if Suzanne had slipped from her horse. Both crossed successfully.

Next came Brian and Brenda. Dick did not worry about Brian, for Brian had proved himself an excellent rider many times. Dick was quite pleased with Brian's abilities on a horse. He had every intention on hiring him during every school semester break until he graduated from the University, if he wanted the job. He was mostly worried about Brenda. He remembered Brenda saying that she had dropped the reins to cover her eyes when they first crossed this way. Dick did not want her to repeat the same steps as her first attempt to cross the slippery slope. He was hoping that Brenda would have more sense and courage with Brian riding by her side. Dick blew out a long-held breath when Brenda and Brian made it successfully across the rocky incline. Now it was his daughter's turn to cross with Effram.

The scorpions started to scurry to the top of their den beneath the soft slate. The constant commotion of movement above their newly developed lair became annoying to all the scorpions. They all scrambled to the top of the slates just as Effram's horse was crossing. Effram's horse's hoof landed directly on top of one of the scorpions, squishing it into the slate. The other six scorpions scattered from Alexandria's horse's hoofs that were trotting over the top of the rocks, they were avoiding being squished. Effram's horse whinnied nervously with the scent of the scorpions and reared up onto its two hind legs causing Effram to lose his balance and was bucked off his horse. Effram landed next to one of the scorpions.

Scorpions tend to run toward their enemy without fear of retaliation when they feel threatened. Effram shook off the adrenaline from his fall and then noticed a scorpion dashing in his direction with its tail in an upright sting formation. He tried to jump up to avoid being stung, but was still dazed from his fall, and couldn't get up in time to avoid the imminent threat from the scorpion.

Dick trotted quickly toward Effram to grab him up from the ground and swing him up and onto the rump of his horse. However, he was not quick enough, and the scorpion stung Effram's hand that was planted directly in the scorpion's path. Just before Dick reached Effram to swing him up onto his horse, another scorpion stung Effram on his right leg. Alex's horse started to squirm, but she got control of her horse and galloped across the rocky incline. Dick grabbed Effram's arm and swung him on the back of his horse.

Alexandria had made it across the rocky slope without any further troubles. Effram's horse followed Alexandria's horses across safely without being stung by one of the other angry scorpions. Everyone watched the scorpions scurry in circles showing their irritation from the disturbance of their den.

Dick placed Effram down on the ground past the rocky incline. Quickly, Dick dashed toward the mule that was carrying the first aid kit. He was truly grateful to remember to pack antivenom for different bites: poisonous snake bites, poisonous spider bites, and poisonous scorpion stings.

"SOMEONE BOIL SOME WATER, QUICKLY, PLEASE." Dick shouted. "BRENDA, FIND SOME SOAP, QUICKLY."

Everyone jumped to action. Dick was worried. One scorpion sting was not a threat, but two is a bit more alarming. Effram could go into shock. Dick observed the symptoms starting to arise on Effram's body. He started to shake in convulsions. He was complaining of the pain and numbness of the two areas where he was stung. There wasn't much swelling in the two areas, but Effram told him that both places had a tingling sensation that started burning. These were regular symptoms, so he wasn't really worried that Effram would die, but he was concerned on how they were going to get him home safely since he wouldn't be able to ride the rest of the way home. Alex prepared the injection of the antivenom shot and handed it to her dad. Dick injected Effram immediately. Someone shouted that the water was warm, and Brenda came running over with the soap. Dick washed both areas, and asked Brenda to bring two rags dipped in cold water. He wrapped both areas with the cool wraps and told her to alternate washing with warm water and then putting a cool wrap every ten minutes for the next half hour. Brenda was the perfect nurturing nurse. Alex was prepared to nurse her boyfriend, but Dick asked her to help the others set up their campsite. He didn't want Alex to fret more than necessary, and he felt that she would be very anxious and overly worried for the man she loved.

"You want us to set up camp by these scorpions? "I asked my dad.

"Sure, we know where they are. They won't bother us anymore. We'll camp over there, closer to the forest edge, not here by the rocks."

I gave out orders to the group, "Okay everyone, Dad says that we must camp here for the night. Let's set up way over there by the forest."

"Brian, Rick, can I see you two over here, please?" Dick beckoned the boys.

"Sure, Mr. Bush," Brian answered.

"What's up Mr. B?" Rick asked.

"We have a problem. Effram will not be able to ride his horse for the rest of our trek home. I need you to build some sort of a travois or a schlep to drag him in. Have you ever seen one in an old cowboy movie? The Native Americans used to use them when they traveled with their injured." Dick waited until one of them acknowledged his request.

"Yeah, I know exactly what you're talking about." Brian whispered, excitedly. His engineer mind was already working on how to build one like the Native Americans did with just nature's supply store.

"Good, I'll leave this little problem to you and Rick."

Rick nodded with approval. "We'll have it ready before we leave tomorrow." Rick offered, hoping that Brian was in agreement.

Dick walked back to the group that were setting up the campsite for the night. He wasn't sure if this incident was concocted by the stranger who was trying to harm them. After scanning the area and not seeing anything unusual, birds were still flying overhead, rabbits were seen moving in the distance, and the sounds of nature were returning for the night, he assumed the horrible incident that occurred to Alex's consortium was a freak of nature. He was grateful it wasn't worse than it was, for it could have been a deadly accident, if Effram was stung by more than two scorpions; it could have been much worse. Dick took a deep breath and breathed in the scent of nature with the smells of pinon nuts, pine trees, and clean fresh air. It calmed his nerves.

In the distance, Buster, the unknown stranger to the Hudson family, lay quietly under the sagebrush. He had to wait until dark before he could leave his hideaway. He was absolutely content with his devious plan and how it turned out. He knew that the Hudson family had not seen him. He also believed that they truly thought that the scorpion incident was a total freak of nature.

Chapter
FIFTEEN

Buster found an isolated area to erect his campfire without being seen by the Hudson group. He moved inward more deeply into the forest, away from his nemesis' campsite. He missed his survival equipment that he dumped earlier in the morning, before his devious plan to harm and maim his adversaries. However, he was enjoying nature to her fullest. The evening was clear and crisp. It was a comfortable night without any bad elements.

Life is finally working in my favor. How unusual, he thought. *Nothing ever worked in my favor before. Nothing good ever lasted in my life.* That evening, Buster fell into a deep and restful sleep. His last thought before falling asleep was, *what am I going to do next?* In the morning, he was still unsure of his next move. *I'll just have to follow them until something comes up,* he thought quietly to himself. He stopped talking aloud for fear that his adversaries would hear him.

As he cleaned up his area, put out the campfire, and saddled his horse, he could smell himself. *I sure do smell rank since my ride yesterday,* he thought with irritation of this new dilemma that plagued him. He kept a good distance from the Hudson entourage, following and spying with his trusty binoculars. He considered his binoculars a good friend. It kept a good eye on his adversaries, and they made him feel secure when he could see the Hudson family, even in the darkest hour of the night. He continued to follow the Hudson group for the entire day, as nothing unusual arose during his stalking of the Hudson family.

By the end of the day, his stench was even irritating him during his trailing of the Hudson group. He couldn't believe how bad he smelled. He had hoped he would come across a stream where he could wash up, but his luck was not that good. However, his luck was about to get better. His stench was attracting a piglet of a very large wild boar.

Nothing unusual happened in the trek home following Alex's group, not until a piglet entered Buster's campsite. Buster knew that wherever there was a piglet, there will always be a female parent wild boar around. His new luck was with him again.

Buster trapped the piglet and placed it into the canvas bag. The same canvas bag he used to carry the seven scorpions to the rocky incline. Now he was carrying a baby boar. A squalling, smelly, wiggly piglet. He listened attentively for any movement in the dark, watching for the parent wild boar. Rustling in the distance, Buster heard the sound of an adult swine calling for its piglet in the not-too-far distance.

His heart started to beat harder. He didn't want to be caught with the piglet. A mean wild boar is more dangerous than a runaway elephant, for a wild boar had long, sharp tusks, and very sharp teeth. They are known for their fierceness. A wild boar will eat meat over vegetation, as javelinas prefer vegetation over meat, and javelinas are known to be a more docile species. Buster was in luck, for this was definitely a piglet of a wild boar. With his trusty binoculars he scanned for any movement in the forest. He could hear the harrowing cry of the female wild boar. The piglet heard its mother's shriek and responded in a tilling chaff. With his binoculars, Buster saw the wild boar charging in his direction toward the piglet's cries.

Immediately, Buster jumped onto his horse and started riding toward the Hudson's campsite, but the piglet was squealing and wiggling so intently in the canvas bag that Buster had to release the piglet. While he kept on riding, he tied his reins on the horn of his saddle, and using both his hands, he dumped the piglet to the ground. The piglet became stunted by the hard fall and became disoriented. As the piglet arose from its fall, it followed Buster and his foul smell into the Hudson's campsite without any squeals. Buster lingered until he heard the parent wild boar crashing through the woods toward the Hudson's encampment. The different smells of the camp enticed the piglet, and it stopped following Buster's foul smell. Buster road off quickly and quietly, undetected by the Hudson group. All havoc commenced as the parent wild boar rushed toward its piglet. Buster got away from the chaos just minutes before the wild boar entered the Hudson campground.

Buster heard the sounds of the wild boar approaching while he escaped on his horse, out of the Hudson's campsite. He heard the squeals of anger and fright from the parent wild boar for the safety of her piglet. He then heard a high-pitched squeal from the piglet as it answered its parents' call. Then he heard the parent wild boar respond with more angry grunts. When he felt he was far enough away from any harm of the parent wild boar, he plopped himself to the ground and placed his binoculars to his eyes. He wanted to view the entire havoc that was about to commence.

Everyone awoke simultaneously. Fear rushed through everyone's blood. The sound of a piglet squealing was coming from their camp, and the sound of a large wild boar was encroaching on their campsite at a very fast pace. Dick looked at Effram, who was strapped to a nature-made papoose, he was out cold still under the pain and sleeping medicine that Dick had given him earlier. Dick jumped out of his tent and ran toward his daughter's tent. Alex was already up and helping Lizza dress quickly. Lizza hobbled toward the horses. Brenda and Brian got to the horses at the same time as Lizza, but Alex ran toward Rick's and Suszanne's tent. Dick saw that one of the piglet's paws was trapped by the tie-down of Rick's and Suzanne's tent. Dick grabbed Alex by her arm and pulled her away from Rick's and Suzanne's tent and pushed her toward the horses.

"MOVE, NOW." Dick ordered his daughter. She ran toward her father's tent to protect Effram. When she entered his tent, she saw her father's gun in its holster by his bedroll. She immediately grabbed the gun. She checked to see if it was loaded and ran out of the tent back into the direction where her father had left her. By the time she reached Rick's and Suzanne's tent the wild boar was already inside. Suzanne was screaming in pain. The screams were horrifying until there were no more screams. Rick was yelling at the wild boar and trying to fight the wild beast with his bare hands; he would do anything to protect his love, his reason for living, his beloved girlfriend. Blood was flying everywhere.

Dick grabbed the piglet and started to run away from their campsite. He was running in the direction where Buster was sitting on the ground. Buster watched with fear as Dick was approaching him with the squealing piglet. Dick released the piglet and ran to the West of it while the piglet kept running toward Buster and his foul stench. The wild boar heard her piglet squeal and started to run toward Buster's direction, and also the same direction the piglet was going. Buster picked himself up, dropped his precious binoculars and began to run away from the piglet. The piglet kept following Buster. The piglet could smell the rancid stench of him. It felt like a familiar scent that comforted the piglet. Buster could not get away from the piglet.

Dick caught a glimpse of the stranger who he believed had been tormenting his group from the beginning of their trek and decided to run in the direction of the stranger.

Alex followed the wild boar into the forest, chasing it while holding the gun in her hand. She had seen her father run in the direction of where the wild boar was running. She had to protect her father. Dick stopped running to catch his breath. He saw Alex running toward the wild boar; fear for his daughter's life enraptured him. He turned and started running in her direction to catch her before she caught up to the angry wild boar.

"ALEX." Dick screamed.

"ALEX." He yelled as loud as he could.

She heard her name, and it was coming from her father from another direction. She stopped running and waited for a brief moment. Just before she was getting ready to follow the wild boar again, she saw her father running toward her.

Dick saw that Alex was carrying his pistol as she was running. He kept on running to catch up with his daughter and yelled. "GIVE

ME THE GUN." He grabbed the gun from her hand while still in a running pace and continued to run in the direction of the man he saw in the woods. The wild boar was still running in Buster's direction. Alex started to follow her father. He stopped and told her to go back to the campsite. "Help them there. I'll be back as soon as I can." Dick watched Alex run back to the camp as he kept running in the direction of the wild boar and the squealing piglet. Just as he was catching up to the stranger, he saw the wild boar spear the stranger in one leg. The stranger flew into the air and landed on his side. Blood was oozing out of the stranger's leg. The stranger was pinned to the ground by branches that had torn from a shrub when he fell upon it. The shrub was blood sticky wet from the stranger's oozing wound.

The wild boar turned to attack the stranger again. Dick arrived behind the stranger. He stood bearing his ground and aimed his gun toward the wild boar. The wild boar kept coming closer and closer toward him and the stranger on the ground. It was grunting and huffing with so much vigor. Dick shot once. It hit the wild boar in the head, but it kept on running in their direction. Dick shot again, and again. Two shots were released, and both shots hit the wild boar in the head. Finally, the wild boar was losing momentum, but it was still coming toward them. They could see the breath of the wild boar. Its eyes were large and furious. Determination to reach the two men was evident on the wild boar's mind. Dick shot once again, and this time it punctured an eye of the wild boar. Down the wild beast went, stopping an inch from the fallen stranger. The stranger cried like a baby.

Dick stood over the stranger and watched the man shiver with complex panic and fear quivering through his body, as the stranger continued to cry. Dick took several deep breaths and shivered with an adrenaline rush that shook his entire body. He froze for several moments standing over the injured stranger staring at the wild boar who lay dead at the feet of the crying man.

Chapter
SIXTEEN

Alex returned to the camp afraid to see what happened in Rick's and Suzanne's tent.

Brian held Alex back and kept her from entering their tent.

"I can't let you in there. Believe me, you don't want to see inside. Please wait until your father returns. Where is your father?" Brian asked her all while holding her tight. She tried to break free to enter and see for herself the damage caused by the wild boar.

"He went chasing the wild boar. I heard several shots. I think he got it. Dad has good aim."

Brenda helped Lizza to the center of the camp. There she directed her to sit on a large tree stump, then she walked over toward Brian and Alex. Brian shook his head to keep her away from Rick's and Suzanne's tent. Brenda listened to his body gestures and walked back toward Lizza. Brian kept his hold on Alex until Dick returned.

They all watched Dick helping a wounded stranger into their camp. Everyone seemed to be still in a cautious alert.

"Brian, go get a stump or a saddle, something for this person to sit on while I check his injuries." Dick ordered. His tone of voice was not very patient or polite.

"Alex, come here, please. Check him out. Brenda, you've been a great nurse for everyone else here, will you please help Alex with this stranger?" Dick was trying to be kind to everyone, but his adrenaline was scaling higher than his blood pressure could take. He had to sit for a minute to gather his composure. While he sat on the ground with his head between his knees, Brian approached him and stooped down to whisper into his ear.

"Mr. Bush, Rick and Suzanne are dead. I wouldn't let Alex, Brenda, or Lizza look in their tent. What should I do?"

Dick reached out to touch Brian and thanked him for protecting the girls. "Thank you, Brian." He took a couple of deep breaths before talking again.

"Brian, help me up."

Brian straightened up and then helped Mr. Bush to his feet.

"Don't let the girls near that tent. I'm not sure what to do yet. We need to talk to this stranger and find out what this is all about." Dick turned to address the stranger.

Buster was in a great deal of pain. He gathered his composure to direct all his attention to the group who were all staring at him. He stopped crying and stared at the group that he had hated all of his life. He was bewildered, they saved his life. *Why would they save my life?* He thought perplexed. *These are the descendants and friends of Len Hudson. They are evil people. Why would they save my life?*

"Who are you?" Dick asked.

"My name is Buster Bartley."

"Buster Bartley?" I repeated the name given to us, questionably. I stopped helping him with his wound after he said his name, and Brenda stopped as well. Brenda was curious to hear more.

I felt dizzy with bewilderment. My thoughts were demur. *What is Baxter Bartley's son doing here, now, in the wilderness, in our camp, at night, after a wild boar attack?*

"Yes, Buster Bartley. Your grandfather was my father's partner."

Dick was so angry that he had to hold his fist shut, tightly, until he could control his temper. "Why would you do this to us?" he asked while his voice was shaking with anger. The stranger just stared at the remaining survivors of his dreadful deed. He didn't know how to start with his tale. He didn't know if he should tell them his tale, but the older man kept asking the same question. Why?

Everyone was tense. No one wanted to talk, especially Buster. He had to figure out these people. Why were they kind?

"Did you bring a wild boar piglet into our camp?" Dick directly asked Buster. "Of course not, why would I do something like that? A wild boar is something wild of nature. It comes and goes on its own in the wilderness. How could I manipulate nature?" Buster was ready to deny everything. Just like this young woman's grandfather, who brought his father's deceased body home and said it was an accident in the wilderness. "Did you have anything to do with the scorpion incident this afternoon?" Again, Dick was asking the questions.

"What incident with scorpions?" Buster smiled while denying everything.

"What are you doing here?" Dick continued asking questions.

"I saw you all leaving just after your grandfather died, and I was curious. That's all.

What's the big deal? I've never been in a forest before." Buster stated.

"You've never been camping?" I asked.

"No, I never have." That was the truth. Buster never had camped in his life.

Just then noise was coming from Dick's and Effram's tent. Alex ran toward Effram, she was so afraid that he gotten hurt in all the commotion. When she arrived in his tent, he was wide awake.

"Hey, baby," he said groggily, "I sure am hungry. I feel like I've been sleeping for days."

"Effram, something awful happened this evening. I think Rick and Suzanne are dead."

Alex briefed Effram on the chaos that attacked their campsite.

"What do you mean they're dead?" Effram questioned.

"A wild boar terrorized our camp and went wild in Rick's and Suzanne's tent. Brian won't let me see inside their tent, and there is no movement inside. I believe they are dead."

"Ask Brian if he'll drag my papoose outside with everyone, would you please, Alex. I need to be outside with everyone." Effram asked pleadingly.

Alex called for Brian, and Brian came running afraid something happened to Effram.

"Brian, will you please drag my papoose outside. Please buddy. I need to be there for spiritual inspiration. Alex has been telling me that something awful happened here tonight."

"You bet. Put your hands on the inside of your schlep. I don't want you to get hurt." Brian suggested.

Effram did as he was told, and then Brian dragged the papoose outside. Everyone was so glad to see that Effram was all right. Safe, without any further injury.

"How long do you think I have to be in this papoose?" Effram asked Mr. Bush.

"Probably for another day." Dick answered. "It's for your own good. It's better to keep that leg and your hand protected from any use until the venom dissipates from your system."

"I understand," Effram said. "Alex, would you please get my bible for me. I think we need a prayer before we try to figure out what's going on."

Dick said, "Boy, are you right on the mark in that statement. I sure could use a prayer to figure this mess out."

"Daddy, are you alright?"

"Sure honey, I just don't know what to do with the situation in that tent." Dick pointed toward Rick's and Suzanne's tent.

Effram spoke up authoritatively, "We'll just have to leave it until the morning. It's too dark out now to do anything. Who is this person who is bleeding all over the place?"

"I am Buster Bartley." Buster said listening to everyone intently.

"The son of Mr. Baxter Bartley?" Effram asked.

"Yes, I am the son of Baxter Bartley."

"Has anyone looked at your injury yet?"

"Why would they?" Buster asked.

"Because you're bleeding, and you need help." Effram replied.

"Yes, I am sorry," Dick apologized. "I should have looked at your leg the moment I brought you into our campsite. Brenda, will you help me again?"

"Sure Mr. Bush," Brenda said.

Everyone was becoming very polite and started calling Alex's father Mr. Bush. It just felt right in this chaotic mess.

Both Brenda and Dick cleaned Buster's injury and wrapped it as best they could. There wasn't much they could do for him in nature's environment and with the limited medical supplies they carried on the trip.

"We can't do anything else for him here. We have to get him to a hospital as soon as possible. Obviously, we can't leave until tomorrow." Dick stated.

"Why are you all helping me?" Buster asked. He never had anyone offer kindness other than his wife when he was sick years ago, and he was in a hospital, and she was a nurse.

Just then, Effram lifted his bible to read aloud a prayer to help them through the night with all the evil that surrounded them. A paper fell out of his bible and drifted in the air, down toward the ground right next to Buster's feet. Buster leaned down to retrieve it and stared at the picture that was drawn upon it. No one said a word while Buster stared at the drawing. Only Brian remembered what the drawing was on the paper.

Buster started to cry. He held the paper tight in his left hand, and then he pressed it to his chest, and began to cry some more.

"What's on that paper?" I asked.

Brian answered. "Oh, that's a drawing I did of the epitaph that Len Hudson etched for his partner and friend, Mr. Baxter Bartley. You know, where it said, "Here's where Baxter Bartley departed this land. A gold miner, husband, father, and friend." But you all didn't see the entire etching because it was covered with mud and dirt. Just before we left, I brushed the mud and dirt away and I found a beautiful cross etched into that stone with Baxter Bartley's name etched within the cross. It was absolutely beautiful, and very touching. Mr. Hudson must have really loved his partner to etch that epitaph for Mr. Bartley. I just had to make a drawing of it. I felt that it should be on his burial stone back home.

Buster began to cry again but said through his tears. "All this time I believed that Len Hudson killed my father. I believed that he lied to keep my father's gold. But now I remember, he gave my mother ten bags of gold. It wasn't Mr. Hudson's fault that mother's friends stole all the gold that he gave her."

"You mean you're broke?" Brian asked.

"Broke? I'm dirt poor. I was an orphan at the age of twelve. I've been on my own since my mother died. No one cared for me, except for my wife for about one year. But she divorced me a long time ago." Buster then shared his sad story to Len Hudson's surviving family.

They all watched and listened without any interruptions. Dick, Alex, Effram, Brian, Brenda, and Lizza were all absorbed in Buster's every word. He spoke about how he saw his father's body for the first and last time in its decrepit state at the age of eleven, he spoke about his mother's abuse by thieving men and her death by alcohol when he was twelve, and then he spoke about giving up his son to his ex-wife's new husband, and about so much more. When he continued his life's dreary saga, he began to cry for all the harm he projected upon Len Hudson's family. He felt ashamed of his selfish actions that he pressed upon them. He realized that they had nothing to do with his father's and Len Hudson's actions that were done so many years ago. He was having trouble breathing. His chest was heaving with quick, short breaths. Soon he passed out with the adrenaline and the pain in his leg. His body went limp, and he sat unconscious. Never once did he confess to any harmful actions that tormented the Hudson family on their expedition.

Dick rushed over to check on Buster and told everyone that he would be all right. He may even sleep throughout the night. Then he suggested that everyone return to their own tents.

"Alex, would you mind if Effram sleeps in your tent tonight. I want to stay with Buster this evening. I better keep a watch over him throughout the night. I really don't want him alone with Effram, just in case."

Brian suggested that Effram should stay with him in his tent, while Brenda and the girls can all bunk together. "I feel the girls are going to want to discuss all the chaos that occurred on this trip. They need each other right now, especially since they will all be grieving over the loss of their friends Rick and Suzanne."

Brian and Dick carried Buster to Dick's tent, and then Brian dragged Effram to his tent. The girls rearranged their tent where they could all fit comfortably for the night. Everyone was so exhausted that sleep became more important than the adrenaline rush of the evening's catastrophe. Adrenaline became more of a sleep-producing medicine, a soporific aid. No one left their tent for the entire night, and no one spoke to another person throughout the entire evening. However, each one had bad dreams during their REM sleep. As they all lay quietly in their sleeping gear, the sound of a wild boar piglet was heard by everyone. The squeals of a piglet were endless in the night, as the piglet kept calling for its mother.

Chapter
SEVENTEEN

Back at the Bush equestrian ranch in Glenwood, Mary had a very disturbing dream. It frightened her so badly that she was startled awake. She could not return to sleep. She jumped out of bed and ran toward the living quarters of her ranch hand, Randy. There she pounded on his door until he answered.

"Randy, I am truly sorry to awaken you and your family this late, but I feel there is danger with Mr. Bush and Alex. Will you please help me get the police to find them in the wilderness?" Mary pleaded with Randy, the foreman of all the ranch employees.

"Sure, Mrs. Bush. What do you want me to do?"

"Would you please contact Sheriff Garcia while I go get changed. Explain that I believe that Mr. Bush and Alex's friends are in danger. I'll explain later. I'm afraid that the Sheriff will consider me crazy and totally ignore me. The Sheriff respects you. He just might take you seriously. I want a search posse out first thing in the morning. I'll have a copy of the map route that Mr. Bush took, you can give that to the Sheriff. If the Sheriff quibbles with you and decides not to pursue the search, then explain that I will pay the expenses for the search. Okay?" She waited until he nodded in agreement. Then she abruptly turned, and ran back to her hacienda to change, leaving Randy bewildered.

By the time she was dressed and made fresh coffee with hot rolls for the Sheriff's posse, she saw lights were spinning from the Sheriff's vehicles that were approaching the ranch house. Randy ran up to the Sheriff and shook his hand.

"Thanks for coming so quickly," Randy said.

"So, what's up, Randy?" Sheriff Garcia asked.

"Mrs. Bush is terribly afraid that something happened to Mr. Bush and Alex's friends while they're on a wilderness expedition. I'm not sure about anything else. Mrs. Bush will be down in a moment, or we can walk up to the ranch house." Randy was in complete control. Mr. and Mrs. Bush had always been pleased with his work and his authoritative nature.

"All right, let's go," directed Sheriff Garcia.

Mary was waiting on the porch. She waved at them as they approached.

"Thanks for coming, Sheriff Garcia," Mary said anxiously. She was still shaking from her dream. It was so real. So evil that it frightened her immensely. She candidly escorted Randy and the Sheriff into the kitchen and offered them coffee and homemade rolls. In country living culture, coffee and rolls is an open-door policy for friendship. Oh boy, did she need that feeling of country friendship now.

"So, what's up Mrs. Bush?" The Sheriff asked Mary.

"Please, take me seriously, okay?" Mary pleaded. "I believe that Mr. Bush, Alex and her friends are in trouble."

"What makes you believe that?" the Sheriff asked.

"You're going to think I'm crazy, but I saw it in a dream."

"You what?" Sheriff Garcia said sarcastically.

"Please, believe me. Something is wrong. You must send out a posse first thing in the morning." Mary waited silently for any response from the Sheriff.

"Mary, I can't do that. I can't authorize a search posse unless there is some kind of evidence of a crime."

"I'm telling you there is or was a crime committed. Please, Sheriff, please send a posse first thing in the morning. If you can't authorize it now, then let me pay the expenses, until you get to where they are, and if you find evidence, then you'll be covered. Will that suffice a search posse?" Mary was shaking.

"I guess, Mary, you're shaking. Are you cold?" the Sheriff asked.

"No, I'm not cold. I just know that there is trouble at Mr. Bush's campsite. Please, Sheriff Garcia, organize a posse, and start your search first thing in the morning." Mary was pleading.

"If you're willing to pay, do you want a helicopter search?" the Sheriff suggested. "Oh, that would be wonderful. Yes, please, but it has to start immediately in the early morning."

"All right, since you're paying, I'll call Travis at the airport and send the helicopter out at sunrise. In what direction will he be flying?"

Mary ran into her office and fetched a copy of Alex's expedition route. She handed it to Sheriff Garcia, who in turn, gave it to his Deputy and asked him to make copies, and then to rush one copy over to Travis. "Tell him to leave at sunrise."

Sheriff Garcia organized six Deputies to gather at the Bush ranch with all the equestrian gear. They were ready to leave by five-forty-five in the morning. Mary made breakfast for all the Deputies, the Sheriff, and for all her ranch hands. She was truly grateful that Sheriff Garcia was following through with her appeal.

Mary prayed all night for the safety of her husband, daughter, and all of her daughter's friends. She couldn't stop shaking. She didn't stop shaking until Alex's consortium returned.

Chapter

EIGHTEEN

That morning, after daybreak, Dick arose early. He didn't sleep very well, neither did anyone else. Buster was wide awake and lying still in a sleeping bag. He wasn't sure what was going to happen next. He really didn't care. If it were left up to him, he would have preferred to die during the wild boar chaos. He still felt that he had nothing to live for. And the thought of prison life was definitely not an appealing thought. He had lived a hellish life all his life; what was there left to live for.

The entire consortium was waiting by a campfire that Brian started in the early dawn of light. Effram was dragged to the campfire even before Dick arrived with Buster. Buster had to be carried to the campfire as well. His leg was swollen to the size of a New York City telephone pole. No one said a word for quite a while, not until Effram cleared his voice and suggested that he offer a prayer to start the day. No one objected. No one wanted to be the first to say something. Effram's suggestion of prayer was a delightful interim.

After Effram's supplication was completed, Dick addressed the group.

"I've thought about what our next step should be from here. Brian, I would like you to ride alone back to my ranch. We'll all stay here until you can bring the Sheriff of Catron County back with you. We can't leave Rick and Suzanne like they are. Animals would come and feast on them. I can't handle that, and I know that Alex would have nightmares for life on the thought. Truthfully, I haven't a clue as to how to clear this up, and we need Sheriff Garcia's assistance in this matter."

Alexandria asked to be recognized in the group talk. "Dad, thanks for thinking of me. I agree with Dad, but I guess it's up to you Brian to let us know if you're willing to ride alone. You'll have to ride hard and long until you reach our ranch. I believe it's only a day's ride away from here. Am I correct on that, Dad?"

"Yeah, it should be about another eight to ten hours' ride from here depending on how many breaks you take, and how hard you plan on riding. You could get there between four or five o'clock this evening. We've got plenty of food and water for everyone until you get back." Dick stated.

"I don't mind going alone," Brian said. "You all know that I can ride and take care of myself."

Brenda agreed with Brian's assessment of himself and offered a reassuring hug.

"Thanks, Brenda. Will you be all right here without me?" Brian asked, knowing that she would, but he was more concerned with her emotions, her feelings of fear, and the loss of her friends.

"I'll be all right, Brian. I'm the cook for the group. I've got to keep them nourished until you get back." Brenda smiled at him and at the group.

Effram spoke up, "Speaking of nourishment, I'm starving. I haven't eaten for a few days. Please bring me some food."

That set everybody in motion. Brenda and Lizza went to work making breakfast for everyone. Alex, Dick and Brian attended with the horses and the mules. Buster informed them that his horse was tied to a tree just South of their campsite. He asked if someone would fetch his horse. Dick traced off immediately before anyone else volunteered. He didn't want anyone else wandering alone in the forest. He felt totally responsible for the group. And there was another worry that plagued him. The scent of dead flesh would attract carnivorous animals to their campsite. He didn't bring this thought up with anyone in the camp, not yet, but Brian, being a student of engineering, was always one step ahead of Mr. Bush.

"Mr. Bush, can I speak with you, alone."

"Sure, Brian," Mr. Bush walked closer toward him by the horses since Alex finished and went to eat with the group. "What's the problem, Brian?"

"If I leave, you and Alex will be here alone as watchmen over the group."

"I know. What are you getting at?" Dick asked. "I've got my gun, and you know that I'm pretty good. And I have plenty of bullets left until you return."

"Yeah, but there's also a dead wild boar out there, besides Rick and Suzanne's bodies." Brian suggested. "What should we do about that?"

"I would like you to get going. The sooner you leave, the sooner you can return. Alex, Brenda, and I will bury the wild boar. We can dig a hole and roll it in, then bury it."

Brian laughed, "I don't think that Alex, Brenda, and you can roll that beast out there. I went out there and checked on it earlier this morning. That beast is huge. And there's still a lonely piglet squealing for its mama."

"I heard it last night. What should we do about the piglet?" Dick asked of Brian. "Just leave it. If it's old enough to run off on its own, then I think it's old enough to take care of itself. I think the mama just wasn't ready to let go and followed it to our camp. I'm more afraid that a wild cat will hear the piglet and come looking for a meal. That will bring another problem to your campsite."

Mr. Bush stated, "I'm not worried about that. The wild cat will only be interested in the piglet. Don't worry about us."

Brian changed the subject and started talking about Buster Bartley, "Maybe all this chaos was a freak of nature?" Brian suggested. "We can't really blame Buster for an act of chaos by nature. Can we?"

Dick said, disappointingly, "probably not, and we can't blame him for the incident with the scorpions either. But I do believe that he is the person who put the rattlesnake on Lizza's saddle, and then rode off. I'll bet you a nugget from your bag of gold, that he did that."

"No bet. I think he is the culprit for that evil trick as well," Brian said, "but how do we prove it? Lizza can't even remember it happening, and no one wants to bring it up to get her to worrying again. Besides, Buster is denying everything. He claims that everything that's happened is a freak of nature."

Dick asked Brian about Busters life, "What do think about Buster's story? He's had a pretty rough life. I can't believe my father-in-law brought Baxter's body back to his wife in that condition."

"Well, in those days, Len Hudson didn't have much of a choice. He didn't want his partner's body to be left behind without a proper burial. That's my guess. So, he had to bring back his body the only way he knew how. I don't think he thought of it as an evil deed. I think that I would have thought that I was doing the right thing by my partner, if I were in that situation. I'm guessing that's how Len Hudson must have felt." Brian offered his two cents on the issue.

"Yeah, you're probably right on that too. Well, you better get going. I'll keep a close watch on Brenda for you, and I'll watch Alex and Effram. They are my kids. I hear Alex is really smitten on Effram. And Effram has talked about Alex every night in our tent, so, I know how he feels about my daughter."

"Thank you, Dick. I'll see you when I get back."

Dick walked back toward the campfire, but Brian stayed to saddle his horse. He packed his bedroll, water, and some food, just in case he couldn't make it in one day. He strolled back toward his tent and called Brenda. She came running without hesitation. Brian grabbed her and hugged her with great affection.

"I've got to go now. You watch over Alex and Lizza. I have faith in you. You're a good cook, and they need you. Your sense of humor will help them in this horrible situation."

"Thanks, Lover. You're the one who needs to be careful. I'll miss you, but you can bet that when I see you again, you are going to be so very, very pleased." Brenda winked and gave him a seductive smile.

Brian left by 6:30 a.m. He waved as he galloped away.

Dick had to talk to the group to find out what they were going to do with the dead hog in the forest. "There's a dead wild boar just a few yards from our campsite. We can't leave that in the open until Brian gets back. It will attract carnivorous animals. Brian and I talked about it, and he assures me that Alex, Brenda, and I will not be able to roll it into a hole. Any suggestions?"

"We can burn it," suggested Brenda.

"Good suggestion," said Dick, "but I can't see a way to get a fire under it. We don't have any flammable liquid to cover the hog with, so that may not work."

"How about covering it with dirt? Maybe build a mound over it." Buster suggested.

Dick nodded, "Not a bad idea. What do you all think?"

I was thinking of the same thing, just before Buster came up with it aloud. "I think that could help," I stated. "The dirt would smother the blood scent."

"All right, I think that's what we should do. Brenda, you'll have to stay here and be our nurse for Effram, Buster, and Lizza. Alex and I will go dig around the hog and cover it to the best we can." Dick waited for Alex to rise up from her saddle. She had been using her saddle as a stump since we first left.

"I'll get the shovels," I volunteered.

Several hours passed when Alex and Dick walked back into the campsite. They were both sweating excessively.

Brenda announced, "you guys' stink, and you too Mr. Baxter. All three of you, stink. I'll boil some water and get the soap. You three are going to wash up. That's an order. Effram, Lizza, and I shouldn't have to suffer with your stench."

They all laughed, even Buster. Buster still couldn't believe that they were treating him like he were a member of their group. He wasn't complaining. He's just never felt comradeship with anyone before.

Brenda gave orders, "And I want your stinky clothes too. I'll boil them in another pot and let them soak for a bit before I wash them."

Buster said, "Madam, I don't have any other clothes to put on."

"Oh, please, don't call me madam, my name is Brenda."

"Brenda, I can't take my clothes off. I don't have anything else to wear."

Effram suggested, "I've brought plenty of slacks. I think they'll suit you. I can only wear one pair at a time."

"Are you sure, sir?" Buster questioned.

"My name is Effram, not sir."

"Okay, Effram. Thank you for the loan of your pants." Buster announced, again bewildered by their kindness.

Dick was not going to offer any of his clothes. He was still angry at Buster. He just couldn't believe that all the chaos and troubles that occurred to their group were all freaks of nature. He believed that Buster was the instigator of all the catastrophes.

Dick had to help Buster with the removal of his clothes. He agreed with Brenda; Buster did stink. He stunk worse than him. Buster was downright offensive. Dick picked up a long stick to carry Buster's clothes to the boiling water. He stuffed it into the pot quickly to cover the stench. Everyone was watching Dick trying to balance Buster's clothes without touching them.

He looked ridiculous in a very clumsy way. Brenda was good at directing humor in the group. They all began to laugh. Laughter was a remedy to health, so Brenda believed. She kept the group laughing until all three, Dick, Alex, and Buster were washed and refreshed with clean clothes. It felt good to everyone there to have a pleasant moment in the most dire and horrifying situation that they have found themselves in.

It was late afternoon, and Brenda was discussing dinner plans with Lizza when everyone heard snorts and grunts in the woods by their campsite. Effram and Buster were left near the campfire all day. Brenda, Alex and Dick had to roam around to complete the daily chores. Brenda called Lizza to come quickly toward the fire. Lizza was hobbling pretty good by now and hobbled toward the firepit and sat on a log. Dick reached for his gun and checked to make sure it was loaded.

"ALEX, HURRY. GET OVER HERE," Dick shouted. She was still by the horses and mules. She made sure the tether was secure before she ran to the center of the camp.

The grunts were getting louder and closer. Dick cocked the gun and aimed it where the noise was projecting. Lizza grabbed Brenda for security and began to whimper. Brenda consoled her and told her that Mr. Bush had everything under control.

Dick heard her and prayed that he had everything under control.

Effram began to pray aloud for all to hear him. He believed he could keep everyone calm through his prayers. They all wanted to believe in Effram's prayers.

A large black bear's head peeked around a piñon tree. There were several piñons in the gathering where the black bear stood. Dick asked Alex to put some logs on the fire.

"Make it into a blaze, Alex. Put a bunch of those branches on it, NOW. I want the bear to see the flames. The bigger the better."

Brenda ran toward the firepit and helped Alex pile logs in a crisscross pattern. Brian had taught her that air has to circulate in a fire to get a good flame. It worked, the fire rose to a peak in the firepit, but the bear lingered. Mr. Bush started shouting at the bear and everyone else joined in. The bear sniffed and smelt the fire. Fire has a menacing scent to wild animals. They don't like fire and with the excessive noise from the shouts of threat frightened the bear. The bear turned and ran away from the camp. Brenda clapped her hands and hollered, "HOORAY."

"We actually had another freak of nature, and this time no one got hurt." Lizza proclaimed. "I've had my fill of nature. I can't wait until Brian gets back." Lizza continued her thoughts aloud.

Just then, more commotion arose from the other end of the camp. Dick raised his gun in that direction, believing that the bear changed directions on entering the campsite. Everyone was surprised when they saw Brian trotting into the camp, and directly behind him was Sheriff Garcia and several of his Deputies.

EPILOGUE

CLOSURE: A PEACEFUL ENDING

Chapter
NINETEEN

Sheriff Garcia dismounted, scanning the perimeter for any hostile ambience. He noticed a young man strapped to a papoose and an elderly man with bandages on a swollen leg with blood seeping through the bandages. There was also a young woman who had bandages and a tourniquet on her left leg. The air of the camp was foul, like rotted blood.

"What's going on here?" Sheriff Garcia asked.

Dick approached the officer and tried to explain their predicament. "We have a young lady who got a broken leg from being bucked from her horse when it got spooked by a rattlesnake." Dick pointed toward Lizza. "Then there are two men in our camp that have been wounded by freak accidents of nature. Effram here"—Dick pointed to Effram in his papoose— "got stung by two scorpions. Buster"—Dick interrupted his explication to point toward Buster— "got attacked by a wild boar. And we have two dead bodies in that tent over there." Again, Dick stopped to point toward Rick's and Suzanne's tent, "Were attacked by the same wild boar."

"Holy shit! Mary said that you guys were in deep trouble. How did she know?" the Sheriff quipped with disbelief.

Dick asked, "What do you mean, Mary knew something happened?"

"Well, Dick, last night, your wife called me to plead for our help. She insisted that she saw something in her dream. And she said that you and Alex and her friends were in great turmoil.

"She insisted that we start a search posse for you guys. And she also insisted that we leave at first light this morning. She was pretty persistent," the Sheriff bantered.

"Bless my Mary," Dick exclaimed with deep appreciation for his wife's intuitive nature.

"You bet," Effram said in a gratitude of prayer. "Bless Mary, mother of God, that she was in tune with the Holy Spirit and with your Mary."

No one was going to argue with Effram. It could have been his prayers that touched Mary's intuition. No one would have ever denied Effram's faith. Effram's faith may have strengthened everyone else's faith in the Hudson family camp, even Buster Bartley. The sheriff walked over toward Rick's and Suzanne's tent. He poked his head past the entrance flap, and quickly pulled it out. "Did any of you look in there to see if they were still alive?"

Brian stepped up after dismounting, "I did," he said. I knew they were dead. I reached in to check for a pulse from the front to check on Rick. I didn't get a pulse. Then I went around to the back and reached in from the drainage flap, I did not get a pulse on Suzanne from her wrist that was against the back wall. I told Mr. Bush that they were both dead and that I wouldn't let the girls see their friends in that condition. So, unless Mr. Bush looked in, I am the only one who proclaimed their death. I did receive an EMT certificate from the University last year."

"After Brian told me that they were dead, I didn't go in to see the kids that way." Dick stated. "And there was so much to do out here to keep the rest of us alive. The wild boar was still running around our campsite."

Sheriff Garcia picked up his radio receiver and flicked it a few times. He called Travis, who was flying a helicopter in their direction. He gave them the quadrants of their position and ordered him to radio headquarters that there are three injured bodies and two deaths at the Bush campsite in the Gila Wilderness. Then he asked Travis to come quickly to bring the injured parties to the Gila Regional Medical Center in Silver City, ASAP.

"Buster, is that your name?" Sheriff Garcia asked, "I believe that you are in need of some serious medical attention. Our emergency evacuation helicopter will be here presently. We are going to put you on it first and get you some help. Please lay still until Travis gets here."

Alexandria ran over to Buster and told him that they would hold his ten bags of gold until he is released from the hospital.

"What bags of gold?" Buster asked.

"Oh, you didn't know. My grandfather asked us to go get his and your father's buried treasure, and then he asked me to give you your father's ten bags of gold." Alexandria explained as the helicopter was landing.

Alexandria got up and stepped away from Buster to let the helicopter pilot prepare him for the ride to the hospital. Then Travis walked over to Lizza and Effram and started preparing them for transportation as well. He could transport all three on the helicopter at the same time. It would be crowded, but it was possible.

As the sheriff's deputies were lifting Buster to escort him to the helicopter, Alex shouted, "YOU'RE RICH, MR. BARTLEY. EXTRAVAGANTLY, RICH!"

How could this be? Buster pondered this turn of events in his life. A miracle given to him by the family that he hated all his life. Oh yes, he would ponder this quandary all the way to the Gila Regional Medical Center in Silver City and for the rest of his life. That day, Buster began to pray.

Brian and Brenda volunteered to help Alex and her father bring the horses, mules and gold back to the ranch. Brenda realized that it was only one more day's ride back to the ranch, and now she considered herself a genuine cowgirl. She earned it, sore ass in all, even though she still had trouble mounting her horse.

Alex and Brenda walked Lizza toward the helicopter. All of them group-hugged, and they promised to visit Lizza as soon as they returned the animals to the Bush ranch.

The girls offered to go with Alex to talk with Suzanne's parents about the death of their daughter and her boyfriend, Rick. Alex declined their kind offer and told them that she would rather handle that delicate problem alone. However, Mr. Bush had a similar offer and refused to let Alexandria deal with that sensitive matter alone. Both Mr. and Mrs. Bush supported Alex in that very painful mission. They were worried about their daughter, Alexandria, for she too lost two dear companions and was dealing with the emotional struggles that was impelled upon her by her grandfather, Len Hudson, when he asked her to accept his quest on his dying bed.

Alex insisted that Suzanne's and Rick's parents receive their bags of gold. Not that a bag of gold could ever replace her friends.

THE END

The Day I Met
Tony Hillerman

Poem by Annmarie H. Pearson

One day, many moons ago, in Santa Fe, New Mexico
I met the famous author Tony Hillerman, the writer
of detective novels of Navajo mysteries.
I was invited to travel a spell from Los Lunas,
New Mexico, with my dear friend Bahni Kaye,
to an unknown home in Santa Fe.
Bahni, you see, was a novice writer, and she
was always encouraging me to succeed.
She had been invited to join a critique group of local
authors with a spirited passion for writing.
We sat in a circle in the home of the unknown, waiting
for the host to begin. I sat alone for a time.
Bahni, my traveling companion, sat to my left, and after a while,
Mr. Hillerman took the seat to my right. Bahni looked over at
me, and since she is six-foot-one and I am only four-foot-eight,
she had no trouble eyeing Mr. Hillerman over me.
He smiled at her and then looked down toward me. The group
commenced, and stories were told. We each had to describe a
book that was forming in our mind's eye. It was my turn,
and I shared the story of *Alexandria's Gold*.
Time had come for the circle to end, but it did not end there for me.
Mr. Hillerman returned to his seat by my side,
and addressed me directly, eye to eye.
He told me he was looking to help a
newcomer, a greenhorn, an amateur,

and that exactly described me.
He liked my story, he said to me, and offered to help it along.
My heart palpated with delight, but soon it became forlorn.
"I am the mother of two boys and a wife to their father," I said.
Then I took a deep breath and continued to say,
"I work a forty-hour job, and I am my son's homeroom mother.
I am a student that is taking classes at night, and I
had to travel two hours to be here tonight.
I cannot see how this can work out." And
there I ended my bleak discourse.
Mr. Hillerman touched my hand and smiled kindly at me.
"I wish you luck when you are ready to write,"
he said, so polite, as he stood up
and slowly walked toward another.
My heart flustered a beat as I put on my coat to depart.
Bahni was excited about the evening's events and
talked most of the way homeward bound.
It took another two hours to return to our homes as we
were still ninety long miles down the road to go.
I never returned to the unknown home in Santa
Fe, and I never met Mr. Hillerman again.
After publishing several mysteries of my own
and still an avid Hillerman fan,
today I smile and reminisce on
the Day I Met Tony Hillerman.

www.ingramcontent.com/pod-product-compliance
Lightning Source LLC
LaVergne TN
LVHW011708060526
838200LV00051B/2817